W9-BGJ-327

"Who are those people?" Lauren asked,

holding her placard aloft as she and the other members of the Progressive Student's Coalition headed to their protest destination.

A dark line of people was marching toward them, their formation as purposeful as the coalition's.

Lauren began to tremble when she noticed that the people were in uniform. As they stomped closer, she saw their riot helmets and threatening wooden sticks.

"Police!" she yelled.

"Campus security," said someone else.

"How did they know we were coming?"

"It's like they were waiting for us," Dash swore.

"Freeze, all of you," the head office ordered.

Don't miss these books in the exciting FRESHMAN DORM series

And, coming soon . . .

FRESHMAN GUYS

LINDA A. COONEY

HarperPaperbacks
A Division of HarperCollinsPublishers

If you purchased this book without a cover, you should be aware that this book is stolen property. It was reported as "unsold and destroyed" to the publisher and neither the author nor the publisher has received any payment for this "stripped book."

This is a work of fiction. The characters, incidents, and dialogues are products of the author's imagination and are not to be construed as real. Any resemblance to actual events or persons, living or dead, is entirely coincidental.

HarperPaperbacks   *A Division of* HarperCollins*Publishers*
10 East 53rd Street, New York, N.Y. 10022

Copyright © 1990 by Linda Alper and Kevin Cooney
All rights reserved. No part of this book may be used or reproduced in any manner whatsoever without written permission of the publisher, except in the case of brief quotations embodied in critical articles and reviews. For information address HarperCollins*Publishers*,
10 East 53rd Street, New York, N.Y. 10022

Cover art by Tony Greco

First HarperPaperbacks printing: November 1990

Printed in the United States of America

HarperPaperbacks and colophon are trademarks of HarperCollins*Publishers*

10 9 8 7 6 5

One

•••••••••••••

Lauren sneaked down to the basement of Coleridge Hall. For once, there were no student movies being shot in the creative-arts dorm, and no modern dances being rehearsed. The only sounds came from the humming soda machines and a washing machine on spin.

Lauren padded across the concrete floor, passing rows and rows of student mailboxes, and picked up the receiver of the pay phone. Quickly, she took out her telephone credit card, punched the East Coast number and then the number of her card.

"Turnbell-Smythe residence."

"It's me, Mrs. Bailey," Lauren told the house-keeper. "Is my mother home?"

"Your mother is getting ready for the hospital charity luncheon, dear. Hold on. I'll get her."

Lauren waited while footsteps echoed down a long hall. A few minutes later, she heard her mother's brittle, well-bred voice.

"Lauren, what's wrong?" demanded Mrs. Turnbell-Smythe.

"Nothing's wrong!" Lauren lied, hugging her soft middle.

"Then why are you calling?"

"I need to discuss something with you." Lauren drew a deep breath. "Something important."

"Well." Her mother clucked. "Have you finally come to your senses?"

Lauren cringed.

"Lauren, I told you that creative-writing program wouldn't be worth putting up with a state university in the West. I just hope your father can still get you into a private school back here."

"Mother, that's not it. I like the creative-writing program. I even submitted an article to the campus newspaper."

"Is it that dreadful dorm?"

"It's not the dorm! And it's not my roommate.

Faith is really nice." Lauren glanced around to make sure that she was still alone.

"Then what is it?"

"It's, well . . . uh . . . the sorority. The Tri Betas."

There was an icy pause. "What about the Tri Betas? I thought they offered you a bid. They invited you to join."

"They did."

"So what's the problem?"

Lauren wasn't sure how to explain it. *Mother, they think I'm a shy, fat dud. The only reason they asked me to pledge is because you were a Tri Beta and donated money to their house.* "I . . . well, I don't think I fit in."

"Of course you do."

"Mother, will you listen to me for once? The Tri Beta sisters are all beautiful and social and—" Lauren froze. She thought she'd heard feet clomping down the basement stairs. She waited. No one appeared.

"And that's exactly why you need to join their house," her mother lectured. "Lauren, you're a freshman. In another year you'll be able to move out of the dorms and live with the Tri Betas. You have to meet people. You have to stop being such a loner."

"I know." Lauren leaned away from the

phone, peering again around the dryers and the video games. "But I just don't think a sorority is the answer."

"And what is?"

"I'm not sure. But I want to find something on this campus that means something to me. Something that matters. Anyway, um, I was thinking of depledging the sorority."

"You were thinking of *what?*"

"I was thinking of quitting the Tri Beta house." Lauren held the receiver farther away from her ear.

"Lauren, why did you bother going through that whole week of rush if you didn't want to join? I have bent over backward to accommodate your silly rebellion. Now it's time for you to meet me halfway. I know you have romantic ideas of becoming a starving writer and living alone in a hut somewhere, but let's be realistic."

"I *am* being realistic."

"You are joining that sorority."

Lauren drew courage from some new, deep place. *"No.* I'm not!"

"If you want us to pay for your education, you are. There's nothing more to discuss. I have to go to my luncheon."

"Mother—"

"End of discussion, Lauren. Good-bye."

"Mother—"

The final response was a dial tone.

"Same to you," Lauren muttered, slamming the receiver back down.

Just then the basement door opened and swung shut. Three pairs of footsteps pattered in. Lauren shrank down behind the dryers as she recognized her roommate's cheerful voice.

"So what is it?" Faith Crowley was asking her companions. "Do you have to deliver the mail through rain and shine, sleet and snow?"

"Earthquakes and volcanos," a second girl added. It was Faith's hometown friend, Winnie Gottlieb. "Through failed romances and nervous breakdowns, too. Or is that the pony express?"

"You two are not funny," spat out a third voice.

"KC," Lauren whispered, crouching lower. She didn't have the energy to intrude on this trio's best-friend closeness. And she didn't think she could face KC Angeletti.

Lauren peered out from her hiding place. Faith looked artsy in a peasant blouse, denim jumper and cowboy boots, her blond hair swept back in a French braid. Winnie wore one of her standard wild combinations: satin boxer shorts, glittery purple tights, and a leopard-print crop top. KC, however, wasn't her usual perfectly groomed, gorgeous self. Her dark curls, gray eyes, and stunning face were half-hidden under a University of Springfield dormitory mail-service cap. She wore an ill-fitting university-issue vest and carried a canvas mail sack.

"Hey, KC," Winnie was teasing, "maybe you should make this new job into your next project for business class."

"Thanks a lot," KC grumbled.

"Why not? You could start your own delivery service." Winnie leaned back against the candy machine and began randomly pushing buttons. Her long earrings danced beneath wild, spiky hair. "Angeletti's express-mail pizzas. Overnight chocolate chip cookies."

Faith put a hand to her mouth to stifle a yawn. "How about singing telegrams?" she suggested. "I could get the other freshmen in the theater-arts department to deliver them."

"You could get the other theater-arts majors to let you out of rehearsal at a decent hour so you could get some sleep, Faith." KC unlocked a row of mailboxes. "You know, you two jokers are not making my new job any easier."

"We're just trying to cheer you up, KC," Faith soothed, rubbing her eyes and simultaneously giving KC a comforting pat.

"Thanks." KC dropped her sack. "This is not

exactly my ideal first step up the corporate ladder. I don't want anyone to see me doing this."

Lauren shuddered. KC was having some serious money troubles, but Lauren wasn't sure why. KC had come to Lauren asking for a loan. Lauren had already bought KC a dress and offered her the use of her BMW to look for a job.

" 'Anyone' doesn't include us." Winnie moved over to the soda machine. "Besides, we're not anyone, we're your best friends."

"I know." KC began pushing letters into the tiny boxes.

Winnie kicked the soda machine, trying to wangle a free can. "Don't be uptight, KC. We'll leave you alone in a few minutes. Believe it or not, I've turned over a new leaf. I've decided to set foot in the library. And I'm not going there to check out the guys. I'm actually going to study."

"And I have to go over to the University Theater," said Faith. "I'm supposed to set up all the props for *Stop the World, I Want to Get Off*. Tonight is our first tech rehearsal. It should only take us about ten hours to get through the show." Faith gave KC a hug, then headed back to the basement door. "Come on, Win. Let's go."

A soda tumbled down and Winnie held it up in triumph. She offered KC a sip, then shared the can with Faith. "Hey, KC," Winnie said, "did Faith tell you? They're selling a bunch of old theater-arts-department costumes this week in the fine-arts complex. I'm sure it will be just my style. Three-cornered hats. Gorilla suits. Togas. We all have to go."

"That's just what my image needs—more grungy clothes that have already been sweated in by a dozen other freshmen." KC gestured to her cap and vest. "This is the opposite of dress-for-success. It's more like dress-for-disaster."

"You look swell." Winnie bobbed back over to KC, kissed the top of her head, then began to follow Faith up the stairs. "We should tell Lauren about the sale, too. Maybe she'll want to join us."

KC flinched at the sound of Lauren's name.

"Let's all meet for dinner tonight," Faith called down. "I'll be there long enough to grab three slices of bologna."

Winnie groaned. "Yum."

"See you tonight," KC called. When Winnie and Faith's footsteps had faded away, she went back to her letters and cards.

Lauren sat for a while, feeling like a dorm stowaway. She still didn't have the nerve to pop out of her hiding place and confront KC. So she stayed crouched in the corner until her foot was asleep and she began to worry about being late to English lit.

"Here goes," Lauren whispered.

The washing machine stopped. All Lauren could hear as she crept from behind the dryers was KC slamming mail into boxes and the faint *plunk* of someone practicing piano. For a moment Lauren froze, wishing that she could make herself invisible or beam herself upstairs. Even in that crummy mail vest and cap, KC looked intimidatingly elegant and determined. Lauren skirted alongside the snack machines, hoping to scurry past without being seen.

Suddenly KC whipped around. She gasped. "Is someone here?"

"It's just me."

"Who?"

"Me."

"Oh. Lauren." KC's perfect face turned hard. She and Lauren stared at each other. "Hello."

Lauren looked down at her mid-heel pumps.

"Why are you sneaking around?" KC asked.

"No reason."

"How long have you been down here?"

"I didn't mean to scare you."

"I didn't know anyone was here."

"I was using the phone."

KC's mouth tightened. She went back to work.

Lauren felt sick. During freshman orientation KC had been her closest new friend at the University of Springfield, other than Faith and Winnie. They had rushed the select Tri Beta sorority together. But Lauren had been invited to join the Tri Betas, while KC had not. KC had been rejected because she stood up for Lauren when the Tri Betas knowingly let her be the victim of a cruel fraternity prank.

KC put one letter aside, then moved to the next row of mailboxes. When she couldn't easily fit a small package into a box, she angrily pounded at it. "What are you staring at?"

"Nothing." Lauren looked away. "Do you need some help?"

"It's a little late for that."

"KC."

KC tossed a stray curl away from her eyes. She whipped around to face Lauren. "When I really did need help, you said no. Don't try and make up for it now."

Lauren felt the pull of tears. She wondered if Faith and Winnie knew about what had happened between KC and her. So far, neither of them had mentioned it.

"Anyway, I have this wonderful job now," KC

said sarcastically. She narrowed her cool gray eyes. "I'll be able to get the money I need on my own. At least I hope I will." She rolled up magazines and began stuffing them into boxes. "Lauren, don't worry. I won't need anything else from you. It doesn't matter."

Lauren turned her face away, wondering if anything she did would *ever* matter—if anyone would ever need anything from her besides money. Maybe her mother was right. Maybe she should stick with the Tri Betas and pray that one day she might learn to be one of them. Or maybe she should forget U of S altogether and go to some stuffy private school back East.

KC locked the mailboxes back up and hoisted her mail sack over her shoulder. Before she left, she found the letter she'd set aside and presented it to Lauren.

"For you," KC said icily. "Special delivery. No extra charge." With that, she lugged her mailbag over her shoulder, pulled her cap down and promptly left.

As soon as KC was gone, Lauren held her stomach and closed her eyes. How much of this was she supposed to take? How worthless and alone could one person feel?

Finally she looked down at the letter that KC had given her. It was probably a check from her parents, with the usual strings attached. She carelessly opened the envelope, but there was no check inside. Instead there was a message written on *U of S Weekly Journal* stationery. A charge went through her, followed by a puff of defeat. The *Journal* was the campus newspaper, to which she'd submitted her tryout piece.

The handwritten note was from Dash Ramirez, an assistant editor. Thus far, Dash had barely given Lauren a second look, and so Lauren didn't read beyond the salutation. The last thing she needed that morning was a rejection note.

"Just go to class," she told herself. "Just go to your dumb meetings with the Tri Betas. Give up trying to do something that matters with your life."

Lauren was almost all the way up the basement stairs, almost convinced that nothing in her life would ever work out, when she finally gathered enough courage to read Dash's message.

> *Dear Lauren:*
> *I showed your piece on dorm life to Greg Sukamaki, our editor. He'll be writing you a more formal letter, but I thought you'd want to know that we'll be using your piece in the upcoming supplement for homecoming.*
> *Also—since you're now an official nonstaff*

contributor to the Journal, *you're invited to our annual muckraking potluck on Thursday, one to five* P.M. *at the* Journal *office. Bring a friend if you want. Bring food no matter what.*

    Congrats.

                         Dash Ramirez.

Lauren read the letter over and over and over again. By the time she walked out of the Coleridge basement, she was the happiest freshman on campus.

Two

·················

C was still thinking about Lauren as she rushed out of her Intro to Business class.

"Wait up, Little Angel," Steven Garth goaded, catching up to KC in the crowded hall. His hair flopped over his handsome face. He was wearing unironed khakis and his polo shirt had a Band-Aid plastered over the designer label.

"Steven, why do you always have to call me that?" KC strode faster. She felt like the entire world was after her: first Lauren, now Steven. Faith and Winnie were the only people lately who didn't drive her crazy.

"Because you're so sweet and angelic." Steven

stepped in front of her, one bare foot flapping out of a scuffed but expensive loafer. He bobbed over to kiss her neck.

"Ha ha."

"Little angel is what Angeletti means. What do you want me to call you, Ed McMahon?"

KC tried not to smile as she shoved open the double doors and walked out into a bright, Indian-summer day. The surrounding mountains were crisply visible against the clear blue sky. The air smelled like sun and grass. "Sure. Call me Ed. And I'll call you Tiffany."

"Call me whenever you want, Angeletti. You were supposed to phone me this morning. How come you didn't?"

"I'm a very busy person." KC hadn't told Steven about her new job delivering the mail. And she certainly hadn't told him why she'd needed to take it. "Back off, Tiffany. I don't have to tell you every little thing."

He flicked his long hair off his forehead. "Why do I have the feeling you don't tell me anything at all?"

"I don't know." In spite of herself, KC nudged Steven with her hip, almost making him drop his books. Then she hugged her briefcase to her chest and ran down the steps into the glittering sunlight. When Steven began to chase her, something inside her lightened up. Soon they were dodging professors and students and a parade of little kids marching into the campus day-care center. They wove past the library and the campus radio station, past Purdy Hall and the University Theater, until KC flopped over, completely out of breath.

"All right, you win!" she heaved, letting go of her briefcase.

"I don't believe that, Ed," he shot back, grabbing her around the waist. "You'll never let me win."

They were at the edge of Mill Pond, a remnant of an old lumber mill, now used for biology research and boating. Steven collapsed on the wooden dock. He pulled KC down next to him, face-to-face. Steven's mocking glare turned softer. He kissed her, and for a moment KC gave into it. She got lost in his warmth, his arms, the crazy way he sometimes made her feel. Then she caught herself and pulled back.

Clutching her knees, KC watched a string of ducks swim. She looked at the treetops, the water, everywhere but back into Steven's insistent eyes.

"So what's up, Angeletti?" he asked, tapping her foot with his loafer. "Don't push this hide-

and-seek stage too far. I thought we had gotten past this. Remember, we're business partners."

"I know."

"We're a team."

"Okay."

"So how come you're still running away from me?"

Part of KC wanted to keep running forever. Yet another part wanted to tell Steven everything. "Don't ask, you spoiled brat. You don't really want to know."

"Whatever you say, Ed." He shook his Rolex watch and squinted into the sun. "So let's talk about business class."

KC stiffened. She and Steven were working on a business-class project, supplying shirts to the intramural dorm soccer teams. "What about it?"

"Bernhard's Wholesale Athletic Supply called me this morning. They'll have the shirts ready two weeks from this Monday. They want cash when we pick them up."

KC's heart began to pound.

"Do you want to take care of that?"

"Sure. Why not?"

Steven leaned toward the pond, then flicked water at her. "If you want me to help with the banking, just say so. You don't have to do everything yourself."

"It's under control," KC answered quickly.

"You're too under control, Angeletti. That's what scares me. I like you better when you're a little more out of control."

KC thought back to the past weekend, when she'd realized what she'd done—taking money that wasn't hers, money they'd collected on the shirts—and felt so scared that she'd fallen into his arms, weeping, embracing, kissing on the muddy dorm green. Thank God she wasn't the type of girl who blushed. "Give me a break, Garth."

He blew against the back of her neck. "I give you nothing but breaks, Little Angel."

KC buried her face in her hands. "God, you drive me crazy!"

"I know." He laughed. "That's the whole point." Then he leaned all the way back, lounging with his hands behind his head. "So give *me* a break. Tell me something I don't already know. I want to know what kind of woman I'm in business with. My father says you should always know everything you can about your business partners."

KC started to get up and reached for her briefcase. "I told you plenty about myself last weekend. I'm really not all that interesting."

He tugged her back down. "Let me be the judge of that, Angeletti. What about your friends? You said you had two best friends here at U of S. Did you make that up?"

KC wondered what Winnie and Faith would think of Steven. She'd told them a little about him. But she'd left out some important parts, because she didn't know what to make of the whole thing herself. She'd never had a serious romance, and she knew it was crazy to lose her head now over a cocky rich guy like Steven. "You think I made up my two best friends? What do you think I am?"

"You are a mystery, Little Angel. You keep me constantly intrigued. So if these two friends really exist, when do I meet them? When do your friends get to check me out and let me quiz them about your secret romantic past?"

"I have no secret romantic past."

"You have something you're keeping secret."

They locked eyes, and this time KC felt that Steven's blue eyes could see into her soul. She looked away. She didn't want him to suspect that she had anything to hide.

"So, Ed, when do I get to meet them?"

"All right!" KC finally conceded. "How about this weekend? Faith is the assistant director for a student musical, *Stop the World, I Want to Get Off.* If you want to meet her and Winnie so badly, you can go to the opening night with me."

He smiled. "I'll settle for that. What about that girl I met last weekend, the chubby one who owns the white BMW? Will she be there, too?"

KC tried not to react to his reference to Lauren. She stared off at a canoe gliding across the pond. "She's Faith's roommate. Why do you want to meet her?"

"No reason."

"She's nobody important."

"Okay. And what about me, Angeletti?"

"What about you?"

"Am I important? Are you going to bring me home to meet your parents some day?"

"Yeah. Sure." KC could just see her hippie parents' reaction to Mr. Slick, heir to Garth Petroleum. They'd probably tell him to stop eating meat, start eating oat bran, and get rid of his gas-guzzling sports car that was destroying the ozone layer. "I have no intention of going home any time soon. Besides, I don't want to subject my poor mother and father to you."

"Too bad." Steven sat up again and nudged her. "Because I was actually thinking of subjecting my father to you. Not that he's poor. He's coming to Springfield on business in a couple of weeks and I thought the three of us might get together."

Sometimes Steven threw such wild curves that

he left KC breathless. She tried not to show how his suggestion stunned and pleased her. "You want me to meet your father?"

"I want my father to meet you. Mr. Corporate America versus the little angel. How'd you like to join him and me for dinner? You can quiz him on better business practices."

"You really want me to get together with you and your father?"

"Why not?" Steven brushed a loose curl away from KC's mouth. "He's not the world's most wild and crazy guy, but I guess for one evening he won't be too big a bore."

"A bore? I'm sure he's fascinating."

Steven shrugged. "So is it a date, Ed? Or would you rather play more hide-and-seek?"

"It's a date," KC agreed, feeling like she was accepting a dare. "It's definitely a date."

Steven kissed her cheek. "Good. Maybe I'll finally find out a few of your secrets."

KC sat very still, not giving in to his kiss this time. No matter whom she had dinner with, there was one horrible secret that Steven Garth was never going to be let in on. She'd taken three hundred dollars from the Soccer, Inc. account, then used the money to pay off her own credit-card debt. Her only hope now was that she'd be able to pay the money back before Steven found out her secret.

"I don't get this, Winnie. You just sit there watching movies and they give you credit for it?"

"Not just movies, KC. Classic American cinema. The class is called History of Film. I know you think anything I take has to be for total lightweights, but we don't just sit around watching Road Runner cartoons. We have to write critical reviews. Tell her, Faith."

"Don't ask me, Win. I'm a theater-arts major. I'm up until all hours shining a flashlight on little pieces of glo-tape and mopping the dirty stage. It's very glamorous."

Winnie was leading KC and Faith in a jog on the U of S outdoor track. Dusk had fallen, and the overhead lights glared down. Winnie, who was in fabulous shape, set a brisk pace in electric-pink bicycle shorts and a zebra-print halter top. Faith looked thin in her dance-class leotards. Meanwhile, KC wore heavy U of S sweats and struggled to keep up.

"I don't want to major in film, though," Winnie chattered. "I'm definitely still in the undeclared major category."

"Don't worry about it so much," KC said. "You'll find something to succeed in. You're

. smarter than ninety percent of the freshman class."

"Yeah?"

"You'll figure it out." KC slowed down and grabbed her side. "I just wish you hadn't figured out this running regimen."

"Really," Faith agreed. "I was hoping this might pep me up. Now I hope I don't pass out in the middle of rehearsal tonight."

Winnie ran faster. "You'll thank me in time. My mother, the shrink, says that exercise is a key to mental health." She slapped her forehead and ran back, circling around Faith and KC. "I'm a great one to talk about mental health, right? Anyway, most people risk gaining ten pounds during their freshman year. That's a fact. I read it in the *National Enquirer.*"

Faith and KC laughed.

Winnie stuck out her arms and rotated them in tiny circles. "Hey, maybe I should ask Lauren to run with us sometime."

KC frowned. "No thanks."

"I told Lauren about the theater-arts department's costume sale," said Faith. "KC, she wanted to know if you'd be there. Is something weird going on between you two again?"

KC took a dozen strides before responding.

"It's just the same old stuff. You know. The weirdness over the sorority."

"That's what I figured."

"Is that really all? Come on, KC. No secrets."

"That's all, Win."

"Now *I* try to keep secrets," Winnie went on, "but I always end up blabbing. It's against my nature to keep my mouth shut for too long. What about you, Faith?"

Faith looked out at the field equipment on the grassy oval inside the track. Her face, usually so rosy, looked pale and a little drawn.

"Faith, did you hear me?" When Faith still didn't answer, Winnie chattered on. "Speaking of no secrets, KC, what about this Steven Garth wanting you to meet his father? Do you think he'll marry you and leave you his huge corporate fortune?"

"Winnie."

"Come on, KC," Faith joined in again, pasting on a smile. "You barely know him, and he already invited you to meet his dad. It sounds serious to me."

KC shook her head. "It's just a date, you guys. That's all."

"Well," Winnie rambled, gesturing for them to run one more lap, "I think real dates don't exist anymore. At least they don't fit into the Winnie

Gottlieb/Josh Gaffey storybook romance. Page one: Winnie drinks too much and passes out in Josh's room. Page two: Winnie and Josh become just good pals. Page three: wacky Winnie gets her life together—a little. Page four: it looks like Josh is going to come to his senses and ask Winnie out on a *real date,* but instead he disappears." Winnie let out a groan of frustration. "Maybe he bumped his head on his computer keyboard and lost his memory."

KC stopped and flopped over her knees. "Win, how can you talk so much even while you're running?"

"That's how you know you're breathing correctly, KC." Winnie ran backward and grinned at her. "With practice, you, too, will be able to jog and run off at the mouth at the same time."

Winnie raced ahead, sprinting until she tapped the metal fence that separated the track from the pole-vault pit. She waited for Faith and KC to catch up, and soon they were on their way back to the dorms. They walked quietly, past Swendenborg House and the old pioneer graveyard. With the exception of the library and the student union, most of the buildings were dark. It was starting to get cold.

Before they made it back to the dorm green, they passed one more building that was all lit up.

It was a brand-new building, close to the dorm complexes.

The Bradley Computer Center was a modern, boxy structure with a large exhibit area where two abstract paintings were hung. The paintings were visible from the front windows, as was the crowd of people inside, carrying glasses and milling around.

Winnie stopped. "What's going on in there?"

"I don't know."

"Come on, Win. Let's go back to the dorms. I'm cold."

Winnie didn't budge. Although she knew she should be taking KC's advice, she felt stuck to the concrete path. "Would you guys wait for me if I run in there for just a few minutes?"

Faith and KC exchanged glances.

"I thought you weren't going to throw yourself at Josh anymore," KC warned.

"That was five minutes ago." Winnie was already on her way.

"Just hurry, Win," Faith urged. "I have to grab a sandwich and get back to the theater by seven."

Winnie was running again, then pushing her way through Bradley's glass double doors. She knew she was giving in to her old impulsiveness, but she'd been sensible for over a week now and she didn't have much control left.

Inside Bradley she was enveloped by a hundred echoing conversations and the smell of new carpet.

"What's going on?" she asked the first person she saw.

"Marcus Rugstern just gave a special guest lecture."

"Marcus who?"

Before the guy could answer, Winnie saw Josh. She'd guessed that he would be there, and sure enough he was standing with two other guys, pointing at something on a poster. His dark hair had gotten a little longer since she'd seen him last, and when he brushed it back, she saw his single blue earring and the side of his humorous, thoughtful face. He wore an old T-shirt, jeans, and sandals. His leather bomber jacket was slung over his shoulder.

"Josh!" Winnie yelled before she could stop herself.

Josh looked around for a moment, then spotted her. A moment later, he broke off his conversation and shouldered his way over to meet her.

"Winnie!" he said, giving her a big, warm hug.

Winnie melted, letting her hands creep around his slim back.

"I've been thinking about you," he said.

"I've been thinking about *you,*" she echoed. Then she told herself to try and be a little cool.

"I've been hoping to see you."

"You have?" Winnie knew she had to be realistic. Josh lived in her dorm, on the same floor. If he'd really wanted to see her, he could have walked thirty feet down the hall.

"Yeah." He tousled her spiky hair, then retousled it jokingly, as if he'd messed it up. "It seems like I haven't seen you for a long time."

Exactly five days, seven hours, and twelve minutes, Winnie thought. *But who's counting?*

He let his hand rest on her shoulder. "I know I said I'd drop by your room, but a lot has been happening. One of my TAs picked two freshmen to help him work on this program with him, and I'm one of them. Isn't that great? I've been working on it every free minute." He stopped and took a good look at Winnie. "How are you?"

"Fine. Great. Surviving."

Josh grabbed a handful of cookies off a passing tray, then plucked the chocolate drop off one and presented it to Winnie. "I should have let you know I was going to be this busy, but it happened so fast. We're making a game that integrates laser discs and computers. It's really interesting. You know how intense this kind of stuff can be."

I know, Winnie thought. *I know plenty.*

Josh smiled and popped a cookie in his mouth. "Hey, why don't we go out right now? Let's go down to The Zero Bagel. Other than this cookie, I don't think I've eaten anything since breakfast." He lightly touched his forehead to hers and smiled. "Are you in the mood for more truly terrible goulash?"

Winnie was in the mood. The problem was, she was almost always in the mood. She sensed that if she went with Josh now, their relationship would always be one where he saw her when he remembered to think of it. She glanced back at Faith and KC, who were still standing in the cold, waiting for her. "I have reading to do for my honors history class. And I told my roommate, Melissa, I'd quiz her on her anatomy memorization. How about another time?"

Josh looked disappointed. He took a step back. "Okay. I understand. Another time, I guess."

Winnie suddenly doubted there would ever be another time. She was tempted to backtrack, to say, *Sure, you want to stay out all night? You want me to flunk out so I can play pool with you and eat terrible goulash? Of course. Why not?* "Yeah. Maybe I'll see you back at the dorm."

"Maybe." Josh watched for a moment, then

tapped her shoulder, grabbed a few more cookies, and rejoined his friends.

"Right." Winnie stared after him until the crowd swallowed him up. Then she ran back outside to Faith and KC.

"You okay?" Faith wanted to know.

"Was that Josh?" KC asked, staring into Bradley.

Winnie nodded and locked arms with her two best friends. "Let's go back to the dorms," she said. She'd been dumped and led on more than she cared to remember. For once in her overly emotional life, she wasn't going to hold her breath.

Three

"Faith, you are so wonderful."

It was happening. Faith had no control over it. At least that's how it felt. The drama students were finishing up the set for their costume sale, and in spite of her strongest desire to avoid meeting Christopher Hammond backstage, Faith had met him anyway. She'd done exactly what he had asked.

They were together behind the heavy teaser curtains, surrounded by dark velvet and dust. Strong, broad-shouldered Christopher had both his arms around Faith, and was pulling her tightly to him, kissing her on the lips, the cheeks, the neck. Faith felt like all of her senses were on overload, and yet she knew that at any minute some other theater-arts major might stumble backstage and accidentally discover them.

"Faith," Christopher murmured.

Faith felt his hand on her lower back. When she and Christopher were alone like this, they could hardly keep their hands off each other. It didn't matter where they were or what Faith thought was right. It was wild—a ride through whitewater rapids. And Faith sensed it was much more dangerous.

No one knew what was going on between them, not even Winnie and KC. Sometimes it didn't even seem real to Faith. Christopher was a junior, a fraternity bigwig, and a BMOC in the theater-arts department. He was the student director she was assisting on *Stop the World*. And he was also engaged to Suzanna Pennerman, a sorority princess who went to another school.

"I've missed you all day," Christopher breathed.

Faith glanced up at him, glimpsing his auburn hair and square jaw in the dim backstage light. She felt as if her knees might buckle. "You saw me last night at rehearsal."

"Rehearsals are one thing," he said, referring

to the fact that in front of other people they treated each other with professional politeness. "Besides, last night was a long time ago. You look terrific."

"I look terrible." Faith stifled a smile. "I think I'm getting a cold."

"Really?" He slyly slipped his hand under the back of her long hair to feel her neck. "You feel warm to me."

Faith tried to hold back a little. She thought about Christopher's other girlfriend . . . that is, if there was only one. He was so handsome and so popular, sometimes it seemed like half the females on campus were after him. Faith had never said a thing about Suzanna, because she didn't know if she had any right to object. She doubted that Christopher knew she was aware of Suzanna's existence. Before she could even consider mentioning Suzanna's name, Christopher pulled her to him again.

"Faith, oh Faith."

Faith closed her eyes. She felt his arms, his chest, his soft, warm breath against her cheek. Inside her brain there was only one message: *Just go for it. Just go!*

And then she was gone.

* * *

"Close your eyes."

Obedient as trained puppies, the Tri Beta pledges closed their eyes.

"Hold out your hands."

Hand after manicured hand was held out.

"Marielle is taking the basket around. She'll put it in front of you and tap your shoulder. Take a notecard. Inside you'll find the name of your secret homecoming sister."

"Sisters," Lauren muttered to herself. *Secret sisters, big sisters, sorority sisters. What a joke.*

Lauren was sitting in the Tri Beta living room, surrounded by lace pillows, bouquets of roses, silver platters, and the pledging and active sorority sisters. A sorority was supposed to be like a family. For Lauren, this Tri Beta family was about as comforting as her own mother and father back East.

Courtney Conner, the cool blonde who presided over the sorority, continued her instructions.

"Our homecoming tradition for pledges is to pick the name of an active sister and then secretly to do something wonderful for her," Courtney explained. "A pledge can drop by the house when her sister is out and clean her room. She can sneak in and leave her sister a midnight snack. She should help her have the best homecoming ever. No active member will know who her secret pledge is until our party after the homecoming game."

The pledges nodded, as if their heads were on strings.

"Needless to say, this is not an optional event for pledges. The same goes for our homecoming party and the decorating session. Your participation is required." Courtney smoothed her velvet skirt and sat down. "You may all open your eyes now and look at your cards."

The handmade notecards were shaped like craggy mountains, since the sports teams were called the University of Springfield Mountaineers. Lauren ripped off the seal over the mountain's snow-capped peak, then looked to see whose name was inside.

"Great," she grumbled. Her secret sister was none other than Courtney herself. Lauren sank down in an overstuffed chair. There was no way she was going to get out of any of these homecoming events without being noticed.

An explosion of giggles erupted as the tea began and the girls mingled, each hoping to think up the most wonderful favor for her secret homecoming sister.

Lauren stayed put. Of all the Tri Betas, she thought the most highly of Courtney. But the idea of conniving so she could sneak flowers onto Courtney's desk seemed the height of irrelevance. Courtney didn't need any help to have a great homecoming. She probably had more wonderful things happen to her than anyone else at the University of Springfield.

"This is ridiculous," Lauren whispered to herself, still unable to join the other girls. Lauren's younger years had been spent at a series of exclusive private schools. In coming to a big Western university, she'd hoped to finally expand her world. She wanted to do something that mattered, something important. Yet here she was again, required to spend time doing something like waxing Courtney's car and making decorations for a dance.

"Lauren, what are you thinking?" asked a twangy voice.

"What? Oh. Nothing."

"Don't you want some tea?" It was Marielle, with her neat pageboy haircut and turned-up nose, hovering over Lauren with a forced smile. After torturing Lauren during rush, Marielle was now Lauren's big sister, in charge of grooming Lauren for active membership in the house.

"No thanks."

"Are you sure?" Marielle insisted. "Plain tea doesn't have any calories, you know."

"I know."

Marielle parked herself on the arm of Lauren's chair. "I've been meaning to tell you, they're having a color clinic down at Fredericka's, this wonderful boutique on The Strand." Marielle looked over Lauren's wheat-colored woolens, pale skin, and fluffy beige hair. "I went down there yesterday and the woman was fabulous. I thought I'd take you down as soon as we're done here and get your colors done."

Lauren knew the clothes her mother picked out for her were too stodgy and bland. She was also very aware that she needed to drop at least fifteen pounds. But she didn't envy Marielle's near-anorexic thinness, her red lipstick, or her co-ordinated clothes. The last thing Lauren wanted was to be made into another Tri Beta clone.

"Actually, I can't go this afternoon, Marielle."

"Why not?"

"Well . . ." Lauren thought fast. "My roommate is helping with a sale over at the theater. They're getting rid of old costumes to raise money for new sound equipment. I told her I'd go. I have to leave as soon as we're done here."

Marielle rolled her eyes, but before she could offer a snide remark, Courtney took a detour from her rounds and joined them. "What's going on?" she wanted to know.

"Courtney," Marielle began to complain, "I told Lauren about the color clinic over at Fredericka's. But she's going to some costume sale on campus." Marielle smirked. "Lauren, if I were you, I'd avoid the clown suits."

"Marielle," Courtney snapped. She gave Lauren a sympathetic look and patted her shoulder. "Lauren, I read about that sale in the *Weekly Journal*. It sounds fun. We can do your colors some other time."

Marielle glared up at Courtney, then changed her tune. "Sure. We'll do it another time."

Up to now, Lauren hadn't seriously planned on heading over to the costume sale, since she hadn't wanted to run into KC. But she'd just realized that, no matter what her mother said, anything was better than sticking it out with the Tri Betas.

Inside the University Theater, animal heads made out of foam rubber were for sale, along with monks' robes, huge papier-mâché jewels, Elizabethan doublets with ruff collars, faded flapper dresses, and racks of military uniforms.

"Lauren, hi! Have you seen Faith?" Winnie asked as she puttered along the tables of used theatricals, going for a red gypsy skirt complete with sequins and rows of dangling coins. "I thought I saw her for a second when I came in. Then *poof*—she disappeared."

"I haven't seen her," answered Lauren. She picked up a feather boa that had been used in a production of *La Bohème,* smelled it, then put it back down. "I just got here. I had to go to the Tri Beta house first. Um, have you seen KC?"

"Actually, I just saw her over on the other side of the stage. She was so busy staring at something behind the stage curtains that I couldn't even get her attention." Winnie grabbed a pair of harem pants. "Now these are great."

Lauren bit her lip.

"Don't worry about KC," Winnie chattered. "I mean, she's my best friend—she and Faith, I mean—but I'd rather shop for stuff like this on my own. KC will just pooh-pooh all my great finds and stifle my inspiration." Winnie plucked up a wide-brimmed hat and a bowling shirt with *Ethel* written across the back. She turned to smile at Lauren. "You know what? You should try these on."

"Me?" Lauren examined the clothes. She shook her head, then reconsidered. "Maybe I should. I'm going to this potluck party for the newspaper. Dash Ramirez invited me in a note. Maybe I should get something new to wear there. I think I'll feel like a freak in my usual clothes."

Winnie turned to look at her, surveying Lauren's pale, tweedy cardigan and heavy wool slacks. "Don't worry," Winnie said, grinning. "When I'm through with you, you'll still feel like a freak. But you'll *like* feeling that way."

"I won't know anyone at that potluck party."

"I'll go with you," Winnie offered.

"Really?"

"Sure. I'm through with guys who live in my dorm. No more. So if I'm going to stick to my resolution, I'd better meet some other people on campus." Winnie handed Lauren a hat with plastic fruit on it. "I should warn you, though, I'm not usually the one people take along when they want to make a great impression. But if you're up for it, I'd love to go."

"That would be great. Thanks."

Winnie found two long silky dresses, a band uniform, a tuxedo jacket, and a pair of leather chaps. She led the way to the corner of the stage, where several students in various stages of undress were gathered. Once there, Winnie stripped right down to her tights and bra.

Lauren was shocked.

"Don't worry about being modest," Winnie confided. "These are all theater-arts majors.

They're into these public displays." She handed Lauren a dress with shoulder pads and big round buttons. "See how this looks."

Lauren realized that no one was paying any attention. Nonetheless, she turned her back and awkwardly slithered from her clothes into the outfit Winnie had selected. When the dress was finally on, Winnie began adding belts and scarves.

"Maybe I worry too much about what everyone thinks," Lauren said, finding her image in a free corner of the communal mirror. "I worry about the sorority sisters. KC. My mother, who says she won't pay for my college if I quit the Tri Betas."

"That's generous of her." Winnie removed her own belt from her jumper and tried it on Lauren's dress. "That's it. You look great."

Lauren stared. She no longer saw a pasty, overweight society girl. Instead she looked like a slightly hip college student. And maybe that was just how she wanted to look.

"Thanks," Lauren said.

"Listen to me, and who knows where you'll end up," Winnie joked.

Lauren actually admired Winnie's spunk and the way she seemed to follow her own path. Even though Winnie always referred to herself as a mad person, Lauren thought she was admirably sane. "What about my hair?"

"Just do this." Winnie flopped her head over, messing and rubbing her hair with her fingers. When she stood up again, her hair spiked out in twenty directions.

Lauren did the same. "What would I do if my mother cut off my money? I've never had a job. I can't pay my tuition and everything on my own. So I can't quit the sorority."

"Why don't you make them kick you out?"

Lauren messed up her hair some more. It took her a moment to absorb what Winnie had said. Suddenly she stood upright. "What?"

Winnie was staring at herself in the mirror, deciding between the chaps and the harem pants. "Your mom only said she'd cut you off if you quit the Tri Betas. Not if they kicked you out. Right?"

"I guess."

"Then it's simple. Make them kick you out."

Lauren imagined showing up at the Tri Beta homecoming party dressed like a cross between a bowling-alley attendant and a gypsy. What would Marielle say about her colors then? What if it was not a question of fitting in, but of really sticking out? "Winnie, you're brilliant."

Winnie did a little dance. "That's what everyone keeps saying. But I have just one question."

"What's that?"

"If I'm so brilliant, when am I going to stop acting so dumb?"

Faith was still backstage, trying to pair up the single socks and shoes. She was getting a runny nose. Maybe it wasn't a cold, but an allergy. She'd told herself that only neurotic people had allergies, and she'd always thought of herself as boringly sane.

Faith certainly didn't feel sane anymore. She had stayed in the wings when the sale started because Christopher kept sneaking back every half-hour or so to visit her. But he'd gone back to his fraternity an hour before, and since she didn't feel like facing her theater-arts friends, she'd stayed in the dark, dusty backstage area with her odd collection of socks and shoes.

Just as Faith paired up a set of spats, she heard Christopher's voice again. She almost stepped out into the light, but stopped when she heard a female voice answer him. For once in Faith's life, she hung back to eavesdrop.

"So, Chris," the girl asked, "how's it going? When's your musical opening?"

"This weekend," Christopher answered. Faith could imagine his confident, paper-white smile.

The girl giggled. "Is Suzanna coming up for homecoming?"

"Gee, I don't know yet." Christopher suddenly sounded a little tense.

Faith stepped even farther behind the curtains. She felt like the back of her neck had turned to ice.

The girl cooed, "You're still engaged, aren't you?"

Faith couldn't make out Christopher's answer.

"Well," the girl went on, "if you and Suzanna officially break it off, you'd better let me know. There are only about fifteen girls in my sorority who would line up to get a chance with you, Hammond. When you're really free, that is."

Faith made herself continue sorting through shoes. A saddle shoe, a high-heeled pump, a boot with a big buckle, a sandal trimmed in fringe. She tried to find mates for each piece, but she finally gave up. It was no use trying to do anything. She could no longer see through her heavy, silent tears.

Four

•••••••••••••••••••••

*K*C had numbers on the brain. Her mailroom salary multiplied by hours multiplied by days, minus taxes and pocket money for blue books, typewriter ribbons, and pens. The grand total had to come out to three hundred dollars before she and Steven went to pay for those soccer shirts a week from Monday at Bernhard's.

Even while KC was in Western Civ class, the numbers didn't stop. Meanwhile, Dr. Hermann was rolling up the map of the ancient world and putting away his notes. Students shut their books and pulled on their jackets.

"You may want to go over this chapter a couple

of times," Dr. Hermann projected in parting. "There were a lot of ancient peoples running around during this time period and it's easy to get confused. Even historians still have trouble sorting them out. Nonetheless, you'll be expected to be experts by the midterm. See you next week."

KC stared down at her notes. They were marred by mathematical scribblings. "Did you two follow everything he said about the ancient Romans and the early Etruscans?" she asked Winnie and Faith.

Lauren leaned forward to answer, but KC cut her off with a glare. She wished that Lauren hadn't been in the same section of the course as she, Winnie, and Faith.

"I think I followed it, KC," Winnie answered cheerfully. "Between this and my Russian-history class, I'm getting into this old-time stuff."

Faith had already put away her Western Civ notes and was going over a list of things to do for the opening of *Stop the World*.

"Really, Win?" KC said, wanting to make sure. "You followed it all?"

Winnie laughed. "Now if I can just keep from getting mixed up with my other classes, and don't confuse the Etruscans with French verbs, directors of film noir, or Ivan the Terrible, I may get through without blowing out major circuits in my brain. Wouldn't that be a miracle?"

"It would." KC looked back and forth from her textbook to her notes. People always assumed that she was the brainy one. They didn't realize that Winnie was much smarter, and that KC got by on sheer determination. In high school KC had been known to study every day of Christmas break. But between the money she owed on the soccer fund, Lauren, Steven, and the upcoming date to meet Steven's father, KC couldn't keep her mind on her work.

"Do you think we could go over today's lecture again right now, Win?" KC asked. "I don't have my business discussion group today."

"Can we do it tonight instead?" Winnie suggested. "I'm heading back to the dorms to grab some lunch with Melissa, and then I said I'd go with Lauren to this newspaper potluck thing. I could stop by your dorm after dinner tonight, if you want me to."

"I do."

"I'll see you then."

"Thanks," KC said, aware that Lauren was waiting for Winnie. She also noticed that Lauren looked radically different. She was wearing something that looked like a bowling shirt and a pair of pleated pants. Together, Lauren and Winnie traveled up the aisle and left the hall. KC tried not to get uptight about it or feel left out. During orientation week, she and Winnie had wrangled about what was proper college behavior: KC had accused Winnie of acting like a silly teenager, and Winnie had thought KC was becoming a stuffed shirt. They had made up and the last thing KC wanted now was any kind of hassle with her old friend.

Faith was zipping up her book bag. "If you want, KC, I'll go over the Etruscan stuff with you right now." She sighed. "I could use a review, too. I'm afraid I didn't listen all that well. We can compare our notes."

"Great. Let's find a table at the student union and study over coffee."

KC and Faith hurried outside, where the light was filtered through clouds. Everything seemed muffled. As they crossed the main quad, the sun broke through and their shadows appeared on the grass.

Inside the student union, it was all glaring fluorescent light and booming sound. The place reminded KC of part cafeteria, part hip club, and part hip airplane hangar. Banners hung down from exposed rafters. Laughter blasted. The place smelled of hamburgers and ashtrays that needed emptying.

"What do you want to eat?" Faith asked.

"Nothing," KC lied. She was starving, but she could barely afford a cup of coffee.

"I hate to eat alone," Faith said. "Let me buy you something. I got my allowance from home today."

KC breathed a sigh of relief. She *had* to pay back the soccer debt on time, and even an extra thirty cents for a doughnut would be going over budget. She smiled. "Thanks. Coffee and something to tide me over would be great. I'll never get back to the dining commons for lunch today."

"I'll be back in a sec."

KC opened her notebook. Despite the chaotic atmosphere, she hoped she might have an easier time studying in the student union than in her single room in the twenty-four-hour-quiet dorm.

Soon KC and Faith were both wolfing down doughnuts and black coffee. They compared term-paper topics, looked over each other's notes, then resorted to the textbook to resolve the identity of the Phoenicians.

When they were finally done with their review, Faith admitted, "I'm glad we did this. I've been feeling a little fried lately. With opening coming up and all those late nights, there's kind of a lot going on."

"I know what you mean," KC said, relieved to have an opening. Now she knew Faith was keeping a secret of her own, and she wanted to urge Faith to confess, to create an opportunity to share her own secret. She sometimes felt that if she didn't tell someone about the money she took from Soccer, Inc., she might go crazy.

"You do?" Faith questioned.

KC lost her nerve. "I mean, I saw you at the costume sale," she said in a quiet voice.

Faith swallowed. She let her long golden hair fall over her cheek. "What do you mean?"

"You and Christopher."

Faith stopped eating. "You saw?"

KC nodded.

"Did anyone else see?"

"I don't know. I don't think so. I was only nosing around because it was so crowded and I couldn't find you and Winnie."

Faith put her hands to her face. "I can't tell you why, but I don't want anyone else to know about this."

KC finished her coffee, then stared at Faith. "But I already know."

"Know what?"

"About Christopher being engaged."

Faith looked stunned.

"Oh my God," KC gasped. "*You* don't know!

I should have told you right away. I just got distracted by . . . something that happened with the soccer-shirt business. And I didn't know if anything was really going on with you and him. Then when I accidentally saw you and Christopher backstage during the sale, I realized that something obviously was going on. I'm a terrible friend, to just spill this out." She reached for Faith's hand.

Faith squeezed KC's hand in return. "It's okay, KC. I already knew."

"You did?"

Faith nodded and tore little wedges off her paper cup. "Brooks told me. Can you believe that? My old boyfriend was the one to tell me my new boyfriend is a two-timer." She tried to smile, but instead tears trickled down her face. "KC, have you ever done something that you thought might be wrong, but you still kept doing it because you didn't want to stop?"

"I . . . don't know." But KC knew exactly how Faith felt. As strongly as she sensed it was the perfect time to confess her own secret, she couldn't admit to her best friend that she'd stolen money. Faith and Winnie thought she was too strong and level-headed to do anything wrong, and besides, compared to Faith's secret, hers seemed so petty and low.

"I don't know what to do," Faith whispered. "I'm don't think Christopher knows that I found out about Suzanna. It all happened so fast, and we see each only once in a while. At rehearsal we act as if we barely know each other."

"So you've never talked about it?"

Faith shook her head.

"You have to talk about it," KC said, almost to herself. "Tell him you know what's going on. You can't have a relationship based on a lie." As soon as she'd said it, she knew that she needed to say something to Steven Garth.

"I know you're right," Faith sighed, dabbing her eyes with a napkin. "I just don't know if I can do it."

KC stared down at her hands and gave the merest nod.

"Muckraking meatballs."

"That's it?"

"Yeah, right."

"That's our recipe."

"We got it out of the radical students' handbook."

"Ha ha."

"Everything in it is explosively hot, including the Molotov cocktails."

The newspaper staffers laughed. Lauren and

Winnie joined in, even though Lauren wasn't quite sure about the joke. The meatballs had been brought to the potluck by two *Journal* investigative reporters named Richard Levine and Alison Argonbright. Alison and Richard finished each other's sentences and wore identical T-shirts that said Progressive Students' Coalition. Alison had wire-rimmed spectacles that slipped down her nose and made Lauren think of Benjamin Franklin, while Richard had a habit of constantly tugging on his scraggly beard.

"Lauren, there's the food table," Winnie prompted, steering Lauren past Alison and Richard and the others bottled up in the doorway of the newspaper office. Lauren followed Winnie toward a long table that had been set up among the funky desks, mismatched chairs, and blinking computers. The smells of meatballs and potato chips mingled with those of eraser crumbs and newsprint.

Lauren set down the neat pink box she'd been carrying. She didn't want to come off as some pampered airhead, so she'd known not to bring little canapés or petit fours. Still, old habits died hard. In a panic that morning, she'd buzzed downtown in her BMW and picked up a dozen truffles from a swank chocolate shop. Next to the messy casseroles and generic pretzel bags, her entry looked pretty conspicuous. Lauren quickly dumped the chocolates onto a paper plate, threw the box in the trash, and moved away from the table.

She and Winnie shuffled around, sipping flat sodas and feeling out of place. Lauren was relieved to have dressed down for once, even though she felt weird in the costume department's long dress and frayed tuxedo jacket. She kept trying to smooth down her hair and had replaced her contacts with old wire-rimmed glasses. She wasn't sure if she were making Winnie's statement or her own, but at least no one was going to take her for a sorority girl.

Winnie was self-consciously moving to a beat in her own head while Lauren shuffled around, trying to look occupied. "How long do you want to stay here?"

"Not long." Lauren looked around. It seemed like everyone else was trading inside jokes or having heated discussions. She already had the urge to go back to the dorm.

Winnie played with her earrings. "Do you want to walk around? I guess we should try to mingle, or at least eavesdrop."

Lauren tried to laugh. Her feet felt planted to the floor. "I guess I'll just stand here."

"Okay. I'll check out the party on my own for a few minutes. Do you mind?"

"No."

"I'll be back soon."

Winnie restlessly wiggled into the crowd and left Lauren alone to guzzle diet soda and get out of people's way. Lauren moved this way and that, floating on the current of the crowd, until she found herself near the desk she recognized as Dash Ramirez's. It looked as messy as before, with broken Styrofoam cups and stacks of papers. Trying to look occupied, Lauren shuffled a few of the discarded memo slips.

"See anything interesting?"

Lauren gasped and looked up. Dash was right next to her. He plopped onto the corner of his desk, a cigarette hanging out of the corner of his mouth and a red bandanna tied around his dark, wavy hair. He needed a shave. His T-shirt was ink-stained, his jeans were patched, and his voice had an urban street lilt.

She drew her hands away from his papers. "I'm sorry. I didn't read anything."

"It's no big deal." He popped some chips into his mouth. "I don't keep my secret investigative files on top of my desk, you know."

They both stared at the crowd and Lauren realized that he didn't even recognize her. Dash obviously had no idea that she was the same person he'd interviewed such a short time ago. In a small way, that gave her courage.

"Excuse me," she made herself say. "I'm Lauren. Remember, you gave me the topic "Dorm Life" for a tryout piece? And then your editor decided to use it in the homecoming supplement."

He looked at her with a puzzled expression.

"You wrote me a note inviting me to this."

Finally a hint of recognition passed over his face. "What'd you do? Change the color of your hair?"

"No."

Now he stared at her more purposefully. "You look different."

Lauren wondered if she looked like an idiot.

"Better," Dash decided with a sweet smile. He stamped out his cigarette. "You look good."

"I do?"

He stowed some chips in his top desk drawer. "I mean, I'm no connoisseur of women's fashions or anything, but you look normal. You look nice."

Normal was certainly not how Lauren felt. She breathed a tiny sigh of relief. "Thanks. And thanks for showing my article to the editor. I'm really excited about it getting published."

"Yeah."

Then they were staring off at the crowd again. Lauren was still wildly nervous and Dash was probably bored out of his mind. But when Alison Argonbright and Richard Levine drifted by, Dash brightened. The pair separated themselves from a few admirers to join him. Lauren had read some of their work, and admired the two reporters. She stared as if they were movie stars. She wasn't sure if she was supposed to stay or go.

Dash leaned toward Alison and Richard, forming a huddle. "Did you find out about it?" he asked in a conspiratorial voice.

Alison and Richard nodded in unison. Then Alison noticed Lauren and gave her a suspicious look.

Lauren started to leave.

Dash stopped her. "Oh. Richard and Alison, this is Lauren . . . what's your last name?"

"Turnbell-Smythe." Lauren thought she saw Alison's face tighten at the hoity-toity sound of her name. "I've read your column," Lauren gushed honestly. Alison and Richard wrote "Under Our Eyes," a muckraking column on campus and community politics. "I think it's great."

Alison looked a little more friendly. But a moment later she and Richard were ignoring Lauren and informing Dash.

"Okay, Dash, here's how it stands," Alison announced. "I found out that the university regents are definitely planning to tear down all those old houses on Bickford Lane, just off the east end of campus."

Dash shook his head.

Richard took over the speech. "Just because they own that land, they think they can do whatever they want with it. A month from now those houses will be leveled to the ground so that the medical school can have a new parking lot."

"What houses?" whispered Lauren. No one paid attention to her.

Alison continued to lecture Dash. "The people who rent those houses are poor. Some of them are elderly. Where are they going to go after the university destroys their homes? They'll be out on the street just so the med students can have more places to park their sports cars. It's not fair."

"That doesn't sound right," Lauren heard herself pipe up.

Suddenly all three of them were staring at her, as if they'd just remembered she was there.

"Is this public information?" Dash questioned, looking back and forth from Lauren to the reporters.

"It's okay," said Richard. "It'll be in the paper

tomorrow. We wrote an article for the *Journal* about it last night."

Alison nodded. "We have to figure out how to stop this."

"Maybe the Progressive Students' Coalition should work on it," Dash suggested.

"We're already on it. The coalition is meeting about it—" Richard stopped himself when Alison elbowed him.

"It's a secret meeting," Alison said, casting a suspicious glance at Lauren. "We don't want to broadcast the time and place."

Lauren cleared her throat. The thought of people being thrown out of their homes overrode her shyness. "I'd like to come, if that would be okay. Is anyone allowed to come to your meeting?"

Alison looked skeptical. "Anyone who's committed."

Richard looked surprised. "Anyone who wants to help."

Dash looked impressed.

Alison mumbled the details of the meeting and directions to her apartment, where the meeting would be held. Lauren stamped the information in her memory. If only she had the guts to attend the meeting, she might have the chance to do something important, something real.

* * *

Clear on the other side of the food table, Winnie had been examining some old pictures of the U of S campus, photos from when there still had been a Springfield lumber mill and her dorm, Forest Hall, had been a pear orchard next to an open field.

"Aren't you in my Introduction to Film class?" asked a guy who slid in next to her, carrying a small paper plate loaded with little pimiento-cheese slices.

Winnie smiled, grateful that there was finally someone to talk to. "I didn't know anyone really ate that stuff," she said, pointing to the guy's plate. "I mean, I'm no health-food purist, but that stuff looks lethal."

He popped a slice into his mouth. "Classic American instant food." He grinned. "Invented in the fifties. It ranks right up there with Spam."

Winnie wrinkled her nose, then lifted her head to check him out. He was cute, with blue eyes and a soft, pouty mouth. His blond hair was very short, except for a skinny little ponytail that corkscrewed down the back of his neck. Tall and lanky, in karate pants, a black turtleneck, and high-tops, he was definitely Winnie's type. She grinned.

"My name is Matthew Kallender," he said.

"Winnie Gottfried." She cocked her head. "We're really in the same film class?" Half the time the lights in the room were off and they were watching flicks, so Winnie honestly didn't know.

He nodded. "I'm sure of it. Your hair always makes little spikes on the bottom of the screen."

"Oh, no. You should have asked me to take my hair off."

"Next time I will."

They laughed.

"What are you doing here?" she asked.

"I'd like to do a movie review for the paper someday, but since I'm just a freshman, it hasn't happened yet. So I'm doing the classic freshman thing—crashing a party, trying to meet people."

"I'm a freshman, too," Winnie admitted.

Before she could ramble on, he was talking again. "I want to find out about everything that's happening." He rocked on his well-worn high-tops. "I go to a movie almost every night, as long as there's not something really classic going on on campus."

"Like what?"

"Like homecoming. I'm very hip on homecoming."

"I always thought homecoming was one of the more nonhip events," Winnie tossed back. "Those corny parades. And the king and queen are so nice they make you want to puke."

He nodded excitedly. "That's what I mean. The cornier the better. I'm into mythic Americana. So is Steven Spielberg."

"Oh." She laughed.

Together, they drifted back over to the food table, where Winnie noticed Lauren listening intently to Alison Argonbright. Lauren briefly glanced up at Winnie and waved, giving her a serious smile. Then Winnie watched while Matthew tasted a hot-dog casserole and some pink-orange dip.

Matthew suddenly checked his watch. "I have to go in a few minutes—I have an appointment with one of the librarians, who's going to let me look at some old *Life* magazines. But speaking of classic, how'd you like to go out sometime? We could get ice-cream sodas and sing in the rain."

"Are you serious?"

"How about this Friday? I have a couple of free hours after my sociology class and before a meeting of the film society."

"This Friday? Sorry. I'm going to the opening of *Stop the World* on campus. It's probably not classic, but one of my best friends is working on it."

He took an appointment book out of his knapsack. It was almost as fat as a dictionary, with all kinds of compartments and tabs. "I'm all booked up next week. Well, speaking of homecoming, how about getting together then? We could take in a classic tailgate picnic and go to the game. How about it?"

"You mean a date?" Winnie marveled. "A real date? You're actually asking me out over a week in advance?"

"I believe in planning things." His pen was poised over his appointment book. "Are you in the dorms?" He handed her the pen and she wrote in her room number and hall phone number. "Great. We're on for a week from this Saturday. The game starts at four that afternoon, so why don't I come by for you at one forty-five?"

"One forty-five? Exactly?"

"Does that sound okay?"

The trouble with planning so far in advance, Winnie thought, was that you were stuck if something better—something like Josh—developed. But if she spent her life waiting for Josh to show up, she'd be a senior before she knew it.

"Sure does," she said.

"So I'll see you then," he promised.

"And in class, too. I'll try and comb down my hair."

"Thanks."

"No problem."

This is classic, Winnie thought. *Classic and nice.*

Five

....

"**S**o you're the famous Faithful Faith."

"Excuse me?"

"Little Angel has told me about you."

"He's referring to me," KC explained. "Steven likes to call people weird, obnoxious names. It's part of his charm."

"Oh. It's nice to meet you, Steven. KC and I are really old friends."

"Good to meet you, too, Faith." Steven tossed back his floppy hair. "So you're the one I can quiz about KC's mysterious inner life."

"Actually, Garth," KC said quickly, "you'll have to quiz her another time. I think Faith has to go backstage."

The University Theater lobby was packed for the opening night of *Stop the World, I Want to Get Off*. Faith had taken a quick break from her duties to run out and meet Steven Garth, but it was obvious from Faith's clipboard and flashlight, the headset around her neck, and the Post-It notes stuck up and down her sleeve that she had more important things to do.

"Thanks for coming to see the show." Faith said. "I hope you enjoy it."

"Break a leg." KC gave her a hug. "Have a good one, knock 'em dead, or whatever I'm supposed to say."

Faith held up crossed fingers. She made her way through the crowd and hurried out the lobby's side door.

Steven leaned back against the wall of the box office as if he were watching cars go by. He was wearing an expensive tan raincoat over a starched shirt and khaki slacks. His ankles were bare and his loafers were scuffed, but for once, only his coat was wrinkled.

KC snapped open her briefcase and found the tickets.

"Do you always carry that briefcase, Angeletti?" Steven teased. "Do you think you can give the corporate-America image a rest when we get together with my father? I mean, it's okay when we're working on our soccer-shirt business, but if you bring that case along to dinner, my dad might think you're a tax collector."

KC bristled. They could hear the small pit orchestra inside the theater begin to tune up. "I didn't know you cared what people thought. Even your father."

Steven considered for a moment. He grinned. "You're right, Little Angel. I don't."

"We'd better go in." KC led the way to the theater entrance, where she handed the tickets to the usher. She was looking forward to finding Winnie and having her dampen Steven's jokes with equally bizarre comebacks.

"Right this way," said the usher.

Steven followed close behind KC, blowing on the back of her neck as they shuffled along. Finally KC laughed and stopped suddenly, so that Steven ran into her. She playfully poked him with her program.

"So now I get to meet your other best friend, right?" he said, teasing. "You did say there were two best friends."

"Yes. For the hundreth time, Garth, I have two best friends."

"I'm not accusing you of lying."

KC tensed up.

"I've just been looking forward to this, Angeletti. I'm already finding it very interesting."

Interesting was hardly the word, KC realized as she took a few more steps down the aisle and saw Winnie bouncing and waving. *Horrifying* was more like it. Winnie wasn't alone. Lauren was there, too! KC started to turn around. She considered faking an illness and racing back up the aisle. But Steven gave her a quizzical smile and took the ticket stubs out of her hand.

"Over there," he said as he guided her down the aisle.

"KC!" Winnie called out. She was kneeling on her seat, frantically waving. She was dressed in a satin baseball jacket, a miniskirt, and electric-blue tights. "Is that Steven? Hi, hi, hi."

Steven laughed.

KC had no choice. She sidled along the row, her briefcase over her head, her stomach tied in knots. Then Lauren looked up in a flash. Her face went even paler than usual. She pursed her lips and slumped in her seat. As KC got closer, she could see that Lauren had buried her face in the brand-new issue of the *U of S Weekly Journal.* KC felt just as panicked, but she didn't hide. Instead, she reacted by getting even calmer, more collected, and more controlled.

As soon as they sat down, Winnie shook Steven's hand and began to chatter. "I'm Winnie. I can't believe KC has been seeing you for more than half an hour without introducing you to me. Now I've had so many boyfriends that KC and Faith couldn't have met them all, even if they'd wanted to. But KC's another story. Come to think of it, did you know that four guys asked KC to our high-school senior prom, and she turned down all four of them?"

Steven looked over at KC. "Did she?"

For once KC didn't mind Winnie's motor mouth. Actually, she hoped that Winnie would talk nonstop until the lights went down.

"Of course," Winnie went on. "One was Roy Bluntsfield. He was only a junior, so maybe he didn't count."

But Steven was no longer listening. Instead he was staring at Lauren. "Don't I know you?"

KC hid her distress and coolly picked up Winnie's conversational thread. "Well, actually, it was only three guys who asked me to the prom, counting Roy. One guy asked me twice."

Steven was still looking at Lauren. He leaned forward and tugged on the corner of Lauren's newspaper. "Didn't we meet a couple of weeks ago, at a restaurant downtown?"

Lauren glanced up. She was wearing her glasses and a strange shirt that looked like it had been handed down from a gas-station attendant. "Well, yes. We did meet downtown. At The Blue Whale. With KC."

KC was desperate to distract Steven. She didn't want him to dwell on how she'd tried to pass off Lauren's BMW as her own. And she didn't want him to remember how Lauren had marched into that restaurant and set the record straight.

"The guy who asked me twice was weird Martin Sanford," KC continued gracefully. "Remember weird Martin, Win? I heard he went to college in Idaho so he could major in pulp and paper." KC was running out of things to say, but it didn't seem to matter. Steven's eyes were locked on Lauren, and Lauren was staring back.

"What are you reading?" Steven asked her.

Lauren rustled her newspaper. "It's an article by Alison Argonbright and Richard Levine. It's about the university tearing down some houses on Bickford Lane so they can build a parking lot."

When Lauren put her paper down, Winnie picked it up to read the article. "That sounds terrible."

Steven rested his chin on his fist. "What's so terrible about it?"

Winnie shrugged and started reading the article. Meanwhile, KC saw that I'm-going-to-get-the-better-of-you look in Steven's eyes, a look she recognized from their arguments in business class. She cringed.

"It is terrible," Lauren answered nervously. "Those people are going to be out on the street. They're poor. Where are they supposed to go? I think it's wrong for the university to demolish their houses."

"Well, it's not like stealing," Steven said.

KC's heart beat faster.

Lauren got flustered. "What do you mean?"

"The university will pay those people to move out of their homes," Steven argued, his voice quick and cocky. "They'll be compensated fairly."

"How do you know?"

"Look, maybe the college is doing those people a favor. They'll probably get more money for moving than they've ever had before. Those houses are wrecks. The people who live there will get a chance to start over and live somewhere decent."

Lauren's face was turning red. "Why should those people have to start over? I don't care if those houses are wrecks. They're still people's homes. No one should be kicked out of his or her home."

"Aren't you romanticizing this a little?" Steven asked.

"No, I don't think I am," Lauren came back, surprised at the force of her anger. "And even if the university pays those people for moving out of their houses, where will they go? I don't agree that they'll have enough money to get a decent place to live."

Steven sat up. "Then they'll do what everyone else does. They'll get a loan."

"A loan?" Lauren turned her violet eyes on KC. "And how are they supposed to do that? Borrowing money isn't always so easy, especially when you really need it. KC knows about that, don't you, KC?"

After Lauren spoke, her face flushed and she began to tremble. But she kept her eyes on KC until Steven began to stare, too. KC sank in her seat. The only thing that saved her from having to confess about the soccer money then and there was that the house lights went out and the orchestra began to play.

Opening night was a success.

There'd been so much applause after "What Kind of Fool Am I?" that the actor playing Little Chap had sung an encore. And during the curtain call, half the audience had stood up.

Afterwards, the cast and crew partied late. They filled Luigi's entire back room and went through countless pizzas, pitchers of beer, and sodas.

Faith was yawning. She'd worked props backstage, as well as fixing last-minute costume mistakes and distributing good-luck cards and gifts from Christopher. She felt as if she'd just run a marathon. Nonetheless, a gleam of excitement still flickered inside her when she thought back to how well the evening had gone. And that flicker grew even warmer whenever she caught a secret glance from Christopher.

"When the audience kept applauding and the orchestra launched into that encore verse," Christopher was telling Joe, the lead actor, "I thought for a minute that you were going to lose it." He sat at the head of table, looking fresh and happy, his shirt sleeves rolled up. His adoring cast and crew were gathered around him. "I saw this look of horrendous panic on your face. You didn't know what was going on."

"Tell me about it," Joe said. "The first thing I thought was that I'd forgotten my lyrics. For a minute there, I was on Mars."

"It didn't sound like that backstage," Kimberly, a dancer who lived next door to Faith, said reassuringly.

"No one knew," agreed Gretchen, the female lead. "You handled it beautifully."

"Just be sure to tell the musicians not to go for another encore tomorrow night," warned Merideth, the cynical stage manager. "Not unless the audience riots or throws flowers."

Everyone laughed.

Faith and Christopher's eyes locked. The laughter became muffled. Luigi's faded away. It was only Christopher sending Faith a secret message with a wave of his hand and a lowering of his head. He gestured to the back door with his eyes, then pushed away his chair and stood up to stretch his tall, graceful frame.

"Somebody order another pizza," Christopher said in a jolly voice, then patted heads and joked his way along the table until he'd slipped down the hall and disappeared.

Faith wondered if anyone else had noticed that Christopher hadn't gone to the men's room or out to the kitchen to visit Luigi. She waited a few moments while Gretchen and Kimberly stood up and started improvising a tap number. With one last look at the slaphappy crowd, Faith slipped out the main entrance and then walked around the building.

The street was quiet. It was icy enough to see her breath, and a thin layer of frost was on the cars. But even in the cold, patchy light Faith spotted Christopher right away. He was standing next to a car, in a shadow, facing away from the overhead lamp.

Faith ran over to him.

As soon as he heard her footsteps, he turned and opened his arms. A moment later they were together and there was no more cold, no darkness, no night. Faith buried her face against his chest and breathed him in. Then they began to kiss. Finally they broke apart to check if anyone was near.

"Hi," Christopher finally whispered.

"Hi."

"I've been trying to figure out all night how to see you."

"I know." A cold breeze ruffled the back of Faith's shirt. She shivered.

"What a night." Christopher looked up at the dark sky and grinned.

Faith wrapped her arms around him. They kissed again and again until some unspoken message passed between them. It was time to go back, or else risk being missed.

"You know, Faith, when the show is finished, I won't see you every day anymore."

Faith hadn't wanted to think about that. "I'm not going anywhere."

He let her go and shrugged, looking off at the neon signs and dark streets of Springfield. "I just mean that we won't be working together every day. Homecoming is coming up, and that's such a big deal at the frat house. As soon as the show is over, I'll be working a lot more at the TV station. They've promised to triple the hours I work as an intern. It'll be different."

Faith knew what he meant. He'd be back to his jam-packed, successful life. She'd be back to her classes, her old friends, and her dorm. So far their romance hadn't been about real things such as homecoming, internships, or midterms. It hadn't been about words, or plans, or making sense. Instead they'd thrown themselves into a wash of quick embraces and whispered words, secret places, and the constant feeling that everything was going to break loose.

"You mean, it's almost time to return to real life," Faith stated.

"This is real."

"About as real as *Stop the World.*"

Christopher looked worried and touched her face. "Faith, I don't mean we won't see each other anymore. It's just that I'll be busy with . . . other things. You know how it is. It may be harder to spend time together."

Faith realized that KC had been right. She couldn't carry on this romance in a haze of mystery. At some point she had to start seeing clearly. And there had to be some truth, before things went too far.

When Christopher started to leave, Faith blurted, "Christopher, I know that you're engaged."

He froze. "What?"

"I even know that her name is Suzanna and that she goes to another school."

Under the harsh overhead light, his face looked like it was made of stone. "Oh."

"At first I didn't think I cared. I thought that nothing mattered except being around you."

He turned around. "And now?"

"I don't know."

"Faith, what do you want?"

"I want to get together for homecoming. I want to visit you at your frat house. I want you to meet my friends. I thought this relationship was so great because it was different and exciting. But maybe now all I want is to do some normal old routine things. Will any of that ever happen?"

For about the first time since Faith had known him, Christopher looked very uncomfortable. It was clear he didn't know what to do or say.

"Well," Christopher finally said, "if that's the way you feel . . ."

Faith turned around, took a step, and then found herself heading back to the party—alone.

Six

The next week, everyone on campus went into heavy-duty study mode. It was as if the entire U of S student body wanted to get their reading, language labbing, memorizing, outlining, term papering, problem solving and quiz cramming out of the way in time to enjoy a blowout that weekend at homecoming parties and the game.

Even at Coleridge Hall, the singers and pianists practiced scales faithfully, rather than making their usual digressions into rock songs or improvisation. The photo lab in the first-floor bathroom was in use twenty-four hours a day. And everyone involved in *Stop the World* was popping vitamin C and forming study groups to catch up on academic work.

Still, Lauren, Faith, and Winnie continued to meet every afternoon for their soap opera, *The Best and the Beloved*. They didn't pay much attention to the lust and intrigue on the tube, however. Instead, they used the time to crack open the books and study, too.

"I guess KC isn't going to show up and watch this anymore," said Winnie, who lay on the dorm-room floor amidst a mess of homemade French flashcards. She was alternately covering her eyes, checking words, and talking to herself.

Faith was at her desk in a bathrobe, a towel around her hair. A stack of library books sat in front of her. "I guess she's too busy this week between her mail job and the soccer shirts. You know, her soccer-shirt business project is wrapping up soon. The dorm teams are supposed to get their shirts from KC next Monday. I bet she joins us again after that."

Winnie tossed some of her flash cards in the air. "Maybe KC's just busy with Steven Garth. I, for one, thought he was *très* cute."

Even though Lauren's argument with Steven had happened four days before, it was freshly disturbing for her. She wasn't used to arguing with people or standing up for what she believed. "Steven was . . . okay," she peeped.

"I will grant," Winnie chattered, "that he definitely would not mix with your friends over at the newspaper. But that's probably why KC likes him. If there'd been a Young Republicans club in our high school, she would have been the president."

Lauren wasn't sure what she thought about politics. She only knew that confrontation scared her. The argument with Steven had freaked her out so badly that the very next day she'd run back to the sorority. As much as she'd wanted to break away from the Tri Betas, she'd spent all weekend sneaking croissants and U of S pennants into Courtney Conner's bedroom. She'd put her bland, expensive clothes back on and signed up for extra homecoming decorating sessions. She'd even assured Marielle that she would be at homecoming open house.

Winnie took a quick glance at Lauren's TV. "So much for KC. I'll tell you, she's missed so many episodes now, I don't know if I can get her caught up. I can't remember if the father of Sara's baby is Jacob the psycho or that sleazy car thief from California. Can you?"

"I can't remember much of anything lately," Faith admitted. "I love doing *Stop the World,* but

I won't mind it closing tonight so I can think about something else." For a moment she stared out the window at the green, then went back to her stack of library books. "It's been intense. A little too intense."

"Impossible," Winnie exclaimed, jumping up and collecting her cards. "Nothing can be *too* intense." She waited for the soap to end, then pulled on an oversized man's suit jacket and stuffed her cards in her carpetbag. "Speaking of intense, who wants to go on a run with me? Okay, you only have to walk out of the dorm with me. You can just stand in the middle of the green and talk to me while I trot around in circles."

Lauren almost jumped up to say that she would head out with Winnie, since she was going to go over to the meeting at Alison's apartment. But she remembered it was a secret meeting, and didn't say anything. Then she thought about Alison and Dash, and got too scared to go at all.

"I have too much homework," Lauren offered as an excuse to Winnie. She flicked on her computer and tried to think about her latest writing assignment. The theme for the essay was personal courage. The idea made her feel ill.

"Come on," Winnie enthused. "We can make it a journey to the student union. We can run all the way there, and then eat those huge choco-late-chip cookies—free of guilt. Faith, why don't you come, too?"

"I've had enough of your fitness runs for a while." Faith laughed and unwrapped her towel, letting her hair fall down in wet clumps. "Besides, I've got to prepare this report on scene painting for my stagecraft class."

Lauren hesitated, but Winnie was standing over her, pulling her up. "Let's go," Winnie urged. "Too much studying makes Jill a dull freshman. Let's get some fresh air."

Lauren frowned.

"Please. Otherwise I'll end up talking to myself and they'll send me home to my mother for therapy."

"Oh, okay." Lauren hugged her soft middle. Finally she slipped into her loafers. "I could use some exercise, I guess."

Winnie applauded, plopped a baseball cap on her head, and led Lauren out of the dorm.

It was cool and breezy on the green, where they passed the dorm soccer teams doing furious wind sprints. Lauren and Winnie trotted past Frisbee players and homecoming banners that fluttered in the wind. Posters advertising the homecoming dance and a college-president look-alike contest for alums were taped to fences.

Once they reached the edge of the green, Lauren stopped trotting and held her side. "I kind of have a stich in my side, Win. And these shoes aren't very good for jogging. Can we walk now?"

"Sure." Winnie stopped, then began running double-time, circling around Lauren with her knees pumping high.

Lauren was getting tired just watching her. She stared off beyond the dorm parking lot. Alison's apartment was only three blocks in that direction. "How's your roommate, Melissa?"

"I've barely seen her all week. I guess she's always working out at the track or in the library. Either that or she and Josh have sneaked off together and eloped on the sly."

Lauren cocked her head.

"It's a joke," Winnie clarified. "Not a very funny one. Melissa and Josh barely know each other."

Winnie started to head into campus. When Lauren hung back, still staring at the parked cars, Winnie shrugged and began doing sit-ups on the grass.

"You haven't seen Josh lately, either?"

"Not since I attacked him after his computer lecture. Josh likes to hang loose." Winnie exhaled loudly as she sat up. "I'll probably run into him in the hall when I least expect it—when I haven't brushed my teeth and have splotches of Oxy 10 on my nose."

Lauren laughed.

Winnie shook her hands in the air, jangling armfuls of bracelets. "Oh well. I've decided that I need a little more planning in my life. Maybe this Matthew person I'm going out with on homecoming will be the dude of my dreams."

Winnie popped up again and began jogging. But this time Lauren didn't join her. She stayed put, still staring beyond the rows and rows of cars.

"What's the matter?" Winnie asked.

"I want to get involved in something new at school," Lauren murmured, "but I keep worrying about what my mother would think."

"Lauren, don't worry so much about what people think," Winnie advised. "You can't let your mother control your life."

"I know. I let the Tri Betas control my life. I let everyone control my life."

"Well," Winnie advised, taking off in a sprint, "there's no time like the present to start making a change."

"The university regents must recognize the needs of the people."

"They cannot just kick people out of their homes."

There was a murmur of agreement, a few "right ons," and a lot of serious nods. Lauren looked around. Out of the forty or so people in attendance, the only ones she recognized from the newspaper were Alison and Richard, who were at the front of the living room, leading the Progressive Students' Coalition meeting. And she recognized Dash, of course, who looked like he'd slept in his clothes. Leaning against the back wall, he fit in perfectly among the mismatched furniture, the political posters, and fruit-crate shelves.

Alison waited out the comments from the group. "We've tried making appointments to talk to the regents."

"They won't see us," said Richard.

"We've tried letters, petitions, and articles in the paper."

"And so far that parking lot is still going in. We think a demonstration is going to be the only effective way to stop it. Something surprising and dramatic. Something that gets publicized. Something the regents can't brush aside."

Alison held up her hands. "But we're getting ahead of ourselves. To give you all the personal picture on this, I wanted you to hear from someone who lives on Bickford Lane. I'll let her tell you, in her own words, what the university's action will mean."

There was a long pause during which Lauren bobbed up to see what was going on. Richard was helping a thin elderly woman in tennis shoes and a track suit get up from the saggy couch and stand in front of the group.

The old woman fumbled for a moment, then looked right at the students. "I'm Hilda Markman," she said. "I live at two-seventy Bickford Lane." Hilda cleared her throat. "I've lived in that house since I was twelve years old. My mother rented that house from the university sixty years ago and she died in the bedroom upstairs. We've never missed paying our rent. We never bothered anybody and nobody wanted to bother us." She faltered. "I . . . I just don't think it's right that I should have to move now. Where am I supposed to go? I live on a fixed income. The university always charged us low rents. But if I have to find someplace else, I'll never be able to afford it." She began to choke up, then pulled herself together. "I appreciate what you young people are doing to help. All of us on Bickford Lane appreciate it. Don't let them throw us out on the streets. Don't let them!"

Hilda held up a fist, then frowned and went back to her seat.

Lauren had a lump of anger in her throat and the urge to run over to the regents' office right then and there. When she turned back to check Dash's reaction, she saw that he was scratching his unshaven chin with an angry, purposeful expression. Finally he flung his arm into the air and strode up to the front of the room.

"I, for one, think we have to move on this and move fast, before Hilda and her neighbors are out on the street. And I think Alison and Richard are right. Polite methods aren't going to work. I'm not talking about violence, but we need to put more pressure on the regents. We need publicity, lots of publicity. That's why I agree with Richard and Alison: a dramatic guerrilla demonstration is the way to go."

Lauren sat forward.

Dash looked around the room and went on. "As some of you know, this Sunday afternoon there's a black-tie reception for the regents and big-gun alumni in President's Hall on campus. It's the final event of homecoming weekend. And most important, it will be covered by the local news. I say let's give the news station a story to remember."

Dash was answered by cheers. He stepped aside to light a cigarette, then stuck it in the corner of his mouth.

Alison stepped up again and halted the enthusiasm. "I want to warn you all that it's easy to vote for this kind of demonstration, but doing it is an entirely different thing. The last thing the regents want at their posh alumni homecoming cocktail party is a bunch of grungy students telling them what jerks they are and then having to watch it on TV."

Richard joined her. "It won't be easy to get into President's Hall. And if the police get wind of anything in advance, we'll be stopped so fast we won't know what hit us."

Alison nodded. "If we vote yes on this, all the plans will have to be carried out in total secrecy." She looked over the room. "So if you can't keep your mouth shut, stay home on this one."

Lauren kept staring straight ahead.

"So let's vote," demanded Alison.

"All against?" asked Richard.

Lauren's voice stuck in her throat. She could get arrested if she took part in the demonstration. She could get kicked out of school.

"All in favor?" Alison had to know.

"*Aye,*" Lauren shouted, jumping to her feet

and hearing her voice come from somewhere very deep inside.

"The ayes have it," Alison announced. "We go ahead as planned."

Seven

"Heads up!"
"Yo! Timber!"

A long metal bar laden with heavy lighting instruments dangled above the stage. One side threatened to swoop down the end of a teeter totter. Finally it was lowered evenly until it rested on the middle of the University Theater stage. Faith and the the technical crew applauded in relief.

What they were doing was called "the strike." *Stop the World*'s last performance had been the previous night, and now Faith and the techies were dismantling the production. They had to put costumes back in storage, break apart the wooden cubes that had been used as set pieces, take down the lights, and generally clean up.

Faith felt a mixture of sadness and relief as she sorted through the props, deciding which went back to the scenery shop and which could be thrown away. She was sad that her first college production was over, yet relieved to have more time to study, more time for KC and Winnie, more time to think.

But as she picked through the grimy paper flowers, the liquor bottles filled with weak tea, and half-smoked prop cigars, Faith knew that more than the play could be ending soon. She and Christopher would no longer run into each other every day. He would no longer have the opportunity to pull her aside for a spontaneous, secret embrace.

"Yo, Crowley. I found this with the costumes," said Merideth, the friendly stage manager. He had glasses, bunched-up curls, and a cynical smile. He examined an old-fashioned coin purse, then opened it to dump out some fake money. "But I think it qualifies as a prop."

Faith picked up the phony bill. "Is this my tip?" She looked at the money. It was a play hundred. "Hey, I guess I did okay."

"Okay?" intruded another male voice. "I couldn't have done it without you."

Faith spun around to look, something in her jumping with surprise even though she knew it was Christopher. She'd been hoping he'd show up at the strike, and at the same time afraid she would never see him again. But he was there, wearing a white shirt, striped tie, and sport jacket, his auburn hair newly cut.

"You're here," she breathed.

Christopher made a joke of looking behind him. "I guess I am here." He turned back and his eyes lingered on her.

Merideth stared, then scratched his head. In that moment Faith guessed that he knew what had been going on between Christopher and her. She wondered how many other theater people knew as well.

"I can't stay long. I'm on my way down to the TV station," Christopher explained. "They've been arranging my schedule around the musical, but now that it's over they've changed the word *intern* to the word *slave.*"

"It's good for you, Hammond," Merideth teased. "Now you can learn how the rest of us peons live."

Christopher laughed. Then, in full view of Merideth and two carpenters, he walked over and slung his arm around Faith. Faith was stunned.

Christopher started to guide her downstage.

"It looks like you've got everything under control here," he called back to Merideth. "I'll check back later."

Faith and Christopher went down the temporary work stairs and up the aisle. In the dark, they stepped over discarded programs and ticket stubs, finally taking two seats in the very back row.

There they sat close together, knees up. The hammering and hollering continued on stage, but Faith doubted anyone could see them. Still, she was surprised that Christopher hadn't picked a more private place.

"I wanted to see you before this was completely over."

Faith sensed what was coming. The *it's been great, but . . .* She steeled herself for the regretful good-bye.

"I've been thinking about what you said." He paused and watched the stage.

"You have?"

"About wanting some ordinary time together."

Faith knew what was coming. *It's not possible. I'm engaged. It's all over.* "And?"

"And I thought we should go to the homecoming party at my frat house. It's Saturday night. After the game."

Faith wondered if she were hearing things. "What about Suzanna?"

A freshman who had been working on lights jogged down the aisle and Christopher waited for him to disappear into the lobby. "I told Suzanna not to come this weekend since I'm working so much at the TV station." He shrugged. "Other than the party at my house after the game, I won't really be doing much for homecoming."

"And that's why you asked her not to come?"

He mumbled something that Faith didn't catch. For the second time, he seemed uneasy around her. "Well, actually, things haven't been going so well with Suzanna lately."

Faith told herself not to be too hopeful. "Really?"

"We're still engaged, I guess." He turned to Faith and ran a hand through his hair. "It's not so easy, Faith. Our families expect us to get married someday and it will flip them out if we break it off. But then this happened with you, and I don't see Suzanna very often, and how am I supposed to know what to do?"

Faith took his hands. "But when I show up with you at that party, everybody in your frat house is going to know about us. And if they all know, you can bet some sorority girls are going to notice. And if *they* know, you can bet it won't take long for Suzanna to find out, too."

"I know," he said, resting his head on her shoulder. "I thought of that."

"I guess they were serious about this top-secret stuff," Lauren said to herself as she hurried down the stairs to the newspaper office. She'd told herself that if she didn't go through with this, she'd never have anything to write about, that if she chickened out again, she'd never do anything worthwhile.

That morning someone had stuffed a note through the narrow slot in her mailbox door.

LT-S:
Pick up your latest article assignment from D at the Journal *today at four. Remember, this is an exclusive.*

Since Lauren was hardly a *Journal* staff writer, she could only figure that it was some kind of code from the Progressive Students' Coalition. Even though she was due over at the Tri Beta house for a decorating session, she took a detour to the *Journal* to find out what was up.

Dash was at his desk, an overflowing ashtray to one side, a half-empty coffee cup to the other. His usual red bandanna held back his dark hair, and he was scratching a day's growth of beard.

When he saw Lauren come in, he gave her a cautionary look.

Lauren sat down in the chair near his desk. She waited while he proofed an article for one of his co-workers. Then he leaned forward.

She slipped him her note.

He barely glanced at it before shredding it into tiny pieces. "Just act normal," he told her.

The office was noisy and no one seemed to be paying attention to them. "Okay."

Dash kept working, almost ignoring her. Slowly he began to notice her again. He looked her up and down, seeming suspicious. "You look different. Why do you always look different?"

Lauren felt horribly self-conscious. She was back in her sorority woolens, her contact lenses in, her hair neatly fluffed. "I have to go somewhere after this."

"You aren't one of those split-personality types, are you?"

"What?"

Dash took a swig of coffee. "I'm never quite sure just who you are. Where are you going? To a meeting of the Junior League?"

Lauren shrugged.

"Oh, I remember," he sang, his voice lilting with humor. "You're in some sorority, or getting into one. I can never keep track of how those things work."

How did Dash know she was pledging the Tri Betas? She wondered if she had sorority snob written all over her. "What makes you think I'm involved with a sorority?"

"You mentioned it in your article on dorm life. Something about comparing Sorority Row to a Monopoly board."

"Oh, I forgot." Lauren felt like a jerk.

"So why would a sorority girl care so much about a bunch of old people on Bickford Lane?"

"Why should being in a sorority make me not care about things that are important?"

Dash swiveled in his chair. He stared at her, then shrugged. "By the way, this is hot off the press." He handed her a copy of the homecoming supplement, then smiled as she flipped furiously through the pages and finally found her article.

"There it is," she gloated, her delight overcoming her embarrassment.

He grinned, too. "Yeah. It's a good feeling to see it in print, isn't it?"

"Yes."

For a moment they actually smiled at each other. Then he looked around, and rolled his chair closer. "Okay. I guess I can tell you. It's definitely on for Sunday," he whispered. "The regents' reception is from seven to ten. We found a dude in the President's Hall kitchen who's going to sneak us in. So now the big thing is to make sure we don't get caught before we get to that kitchen. We'll let you know where we're all going to meet. You'll get another note." A girl walked by carrying a computer keyboard. Dash paused, swigging coffee until she'd walked away. "Keep your mouth shut about all of this."

"I will!"

He picked up on her indignation. "I already had to vouch for you, you know."

"What?"

"With Alison and Richard. They're a little paranoid, but I told them you were okay. They don't want anybody they're not sure they can trust in on this."

"They can trust me."

Two more reporters hovered, breaking up the conversation once again.

"How do we know you don't go back to your sorority and plan anti-radical voodoo sessions?" Dash asked after the reporters had moved on. "How do we know you don't tell them everything?"

Lauren wasn't sure if Dash was still teasing. "I

don't. They tell *me* what to do. I'm just a pledge."

"Oh, yeah. I've always heard how they make pledges go through rituals and tests. How they make them drink a bucket of bourbon and then walk naked in the snow. Nice stuff." He shook his head. "Actually, it is good stuff—for an article someday. I wish I could see some of it up close."

"I don't think that kind of hazing goes on anymore. It's illegal. Everything now is pretty tame." Suddenly a great vision flew into Lauren's head: her walking into the Tri Beta house with Dash Ramirez. She could just see him sprawling all over the lace pillows, making fun of Marielle, and leaving a trail of cigarette ash. "You should see it, though," she offered tentatively. "There might still be some material for an exposé there."

"Are you serious?"

She wasn't sure if she really was serious, but she could see by the look in Dash's dark eyes that he was. "I guess I am."

"I've been wanting to write an article on Greek life since I joined this paper. On all the sides of the frat scene, not just the side the Interfraternity Council shows. But I'm not exactly the frat-row type. I could never figure out how to get into those places."

This was a great way to finally take Winnie's

advice, Lauren realized. If she were really going to get herself kicked out, to get the Tri Betas to reject her and her mother's money, she would have to do something as outrageous as showing up with Dash.

"How about coming with me to an open house on Saturday?" Lauren mumbled. "It's not a big ritual party, and I'm sure you won't see anything much more dramatic than some ribbons and foamy punch. But it won't conflict with the regents' . . . you know."

His face lit up. "Yeah. Yeah." He scribbled a few notes on a well-used pad. "I can fit that in. That sounds good."

"Really?" Lauren had the urge to backtrack and change her mind, but she didn't. She sensed that if she didn't do something this outrageous, this extreme, she might never do anything at all.

"So do you have a car?" he asked her.

"Yes. Why?"

"I'll be here at the office all day on Saturday. Why don't you come by and pick me up?"

Lauren nodded her head, even though she'd just gotten herself into something else that scared her half to death.

Eight

aith, it's great that Christopher asked you to his frat house. What did I tell you? I'd say that's a definite step forward."

"More than a step, KC. I feel like it's a leap into reality."

"I still think you could have told me about Christopher before this," Winnie insisted. "I'm into reality. Sometimes. And I have been known to keep my mouth shut once or twice."

Faith grabbed the tail of Winnie's leopard-print shirt, slowing her down so that KC, who was lugging her mailbag up from the basement of Forest Hall, could catch up. They could already hear the Forest party jocks gearing up for home-coming. Three stereos competed at top volume, and they were setting up for a beer can–sculpture contest in the lobby.

"I'm sorry, Win," Faith admitted as they wove through the collection of cans. "I should have told you. I've just never been involved in any-thing like this before. I didn't know how to tell anyone. KC found out on her own."

"I guess I'll forgive you," Winnie sighed. She held the door for KC and the three of them went outside. It was after four and there were long shadows on the green. "It must be a little differ-ent for you. It's not like being part of the Faith/ Brooks combo, the most taken-for-granted cou-ple at Lewis and Clark High."

"Really." Faith swung back her long, shiny hair. She finally looked like the old, grounded Faith. Even Winnie's mention of Brooks, her ex-boyfriend, didn't bother her. "I've decided, no more sneaking around. No more hiding. No more secrets. I don't think I'm the type who can handle that in the long-term."

"Who is?" KC snapped. She took a deep breath, then threw her mail sack over her shoul-der.

"What about you and Steven?" Faith asked.

KC cleared her throat. "It's been all business

the last few days," she rambled, not looking at them. "We're figuring out how to pick up all the soccer shirts on Monday and get them delivered to the right people. Plus we've had to write up our report on the whole thing. I'll be alone with him tomorrow night. That's when we're having dinner with his dad. I hope I know which fork to use."

"I'll lend you my copy of Miss Manners," said Winnie.

"You'll have a great time," said Faith supportively. "Your soccer-shirt business is going to be a huge success. You can really celebrate."

KC stopped walking. "I won't feel free to celebrate until this whole project is over."

Faith hugged her, then checked her book bag and headed toward the language lab. "Adios, amigas. See you at dinner."

Winnie kissed KC's arm, then split in the opposite direction, heading toward the student store. "I'll save us the usual table. See you both then."

KC waited until Faith and Winnie were gone. Then she dragged her sack along the grass and headed for Faith and Lauren's dorm.

She could hear the Coleridge homecoming celebration long before she opened the back door. A duo was singing songs by the lobby piano and a jazz combo was improvising upstairs. KC pulled her mail cap lower over her face as she hurried down to the basement, past the churning washing machines, the lint balls, and the occasional single sock.

"Mail's in," sang Freya, the German vocal-music major who roomed with Kimberly in the room next door to Faith and Lauren. She was reading a German magazine and waiting for her wash.

Her companion launched into some old fifties song about Mr. Postman, then demanded in a theatrical voice, "How come you're so late today, O unfriendly mail lady?"

KC ignored them. She was late because she'd worked overtime that afternoon in the mail room, slaving to make up every last penny she owed. And she'd been so flipped out about running into Lauren that she'd saved the Coleridge delivery for last.

Hidden behind the bank of mailboxes, KC took out her remaining stack of letters. On top was a special letter, one that wasn't to be delivered. It was addressed to KC herself, and she'd stowed it with the Coleridge mail so it would be right there, ready, at the end of her day. KC took a moment, tore open the flap, and turned the envelope upside down. A light-green check slipped out.

"Take that, Steven Garth," KC whispered.

She put the check in her pocket. Finally. Three hundred and four dollars for two weeks of back-breaking work. Steven had made an appointment to pick up the soccer shirts at seven A.M. that coming Monday. And despite Lauren, despite her own folly, KC would be there, cash in hand, as if nothing had ever gone wrong.

KC checked her pocket watch, the one that had belonged to her grandfather. She carried it with her as a reminder never to be late. There was plenty of time to get the Coleridge mail delivered, drop her sack and cap back at the mail room, and get to the campus bank. For the first time in weeks, KC's heart beat at a normal pace.

"I won't need this job much longer," she whispered. "Finally I can spend my time doing something productive."

Pushing the Coleridge mail into the boxes, KC thought about Lauren again. When she had first met Lauren, she'd felt sorry for her. Sure, Lauren was the one with the connections and the wealth, but she was so awkward and chubby. Without KC at her side, no one would have given Lauren a second look. And then, when it had really mattered, KC had stood up bravely for Lauren, sacrificing herself in the process.

And how had Lauren repaid her? She'd refused to give KC a loan that probably amounted to less than her panty hose allowance. And she'd threatened to tattle to Steven Garth, to expose everything KC so desperately needed to hide.

The more KC thought about it, the angrier she felt. It made her sick to consider the time and energy she'd wasted making up that stupid debt. She'd almost ruined her business project because of it. She'd had no time to meet influential people or join important campus clubs. For all she knew, her grades would suffer, too.

"Instead of helping me, Lauren practically spit in my face!" KC mumbled. She finished another section of boxes. As if by magnetic attraction, she found herself at Lauren and Faith's mailbox. She selected their mail; a letter for Faith from home and an advertisement from the local BMW dealer for Lauren.

"Gee," KC grumbled, pulling out the key that allowed her to open the section of mailboxes. "Maybe Lauren can go buy another Beamer." When the brass gate swung down, KC could see into each box. And that was when she saw the note already sitting in Faith and Lauren's box.

"Oh, no." Instantly, KC switched gears. She

knew what it was—a secret missive from Christopher to Faith. Obviously Christopher hadn't listened to Faith when she'd told him that she wanted their relationship to be out in the open. KC could only imagine that Faith was going to get horribly hurt.

KC reached for the note, then pulled her hand back. She wasn't sure how far to meddle. Faith pretended to be so strong, but KC saw through her. Under her straightforward manner and sensible clothes, Faith was just as vulnerable as she and Winnie. Besides that, Faith was on the rebound, still recovering from her breakup with Brooks. And yet . . .

KC decided. She had to intrude. She had to do whatever she could to protect her friend.

She took a step back and checked out the laundry area. The machines were still churning, but the girls were gone. Quickly, KC grabbed the note.

"What's this?" KC whispered after reading the message. It was so bizarrely worded that she had to read it a few times before it made any sense. Even then, she was puzzled. Why would Christopher want Faith to meet him in Northwest Park before the regents' reception on Sunday? His frat party was on Saturday night, after the football game. It didn't make sense.

Then KC saw the initials on the top. *LT-S.* Suddenly it clicked together in her head. Lauren. The regents. The argument over those houses the university was going to tear down.

KC read the note over twice more. Although it was subtly worded, she had no doubt about its contents. There was a plan to disrupt that reception, to do something dramatic—maybe even violent—to get the regents to change their plans for Bickford Lane.

What she did have doubts about was Lauren's involvement. KC couldn't believe that Lauren would want to get mixed up in anything so radical. But she remembered how passionately Lauren had argued against the university's position, and thought anything was possible. KC also remembered Steven saying that his own father had been invited to that reception. What if Steven's father were attacked? What if they were planning to kidnap someone, take hostages, or plant a bomb?

KC's heart was pounding. She put the note back, closed up the mailboxes, and hurried to the pay phone. She pulled out a quarter and heard the nerve-wracking *clink* of the coin landing in the slot. When the dial tone came up, she quickly punched in a number.

"Campus security."

For one brief moment, KC hesitated. What if Lauren and the others were planning an entirely peaceful demonstration? What if she was doing this just to get revenge on Lauren?

"Hello? I can't hear you," the security officer prodded.

Well, even if it was only revenge on Lauren, KC told herself, Lauren deserved it. And as far as the demonstration went, it wasn't worth taking a chance. "I have some information."

"What's your name?"

"I can't tell you my name, but I have important information about the regents' reception after homecoming."

"I'm listening, miss. Please go ahead."

"Nice of you to show up, Lauren," Marielle sneered, glancing down from the top of a wooden ladder, her arms draped with sashes of crepe paper.

"What do you mean?" Lauren handed up a roll of tape. "I'm here. I'm helping."

Marielle tossed down a packet of tacks. She had her hair in a kerchief and her nails needed repolishing. Along with the other pledges and active members, she was transforming the Tri Beta living room into an alumni museum for homecoming. Photos covered the walls, along with framed articles describing the alums' fabulous achievements. Girls scurried around with hammers and nails, old yearbooks, and rolls of ribbon.

"I just mean," Marielle said, climbing down, "that you signed up for two decorating sessions but you didn't show up at your first one. We were counting on you, Lauren, and you let us down. By the end of today everything will be ready, so you won't have a chance to make it up. I don't think you can afford to be that relaxed about your responsibilities."

Lauren tried not to gloat. After visiting Dash at the newspaper office, she'd actually gone back to the dorm to write instead of doing her decorating duty. Finally, she'd taken her first step toward doing what she really wanted to do, and irritating the Tri Betas in the process. She only hoped that she would have the nerve to follow with much more annoying sins.

Marielle flopped into an overstuffed chair, leaving the ladder to another pledge and her big sister. She gestured for Lauren to sit on the floor next to her. Lauren sat.

"Did you do remember to do something nice for your secret sister?"

Lauren nodded. She didn't add that she

wished she'd had the nerve to forget intentionally.

"Well, at least you did that. But your clothes," Marielle added in a deadly whisper. "Not that I'm exactly Miss Vogue for this work session, but you're not just dressed down, Lauren, you're dressed . . . weirdly." She picked at her nail polish and shivered.

Lauren was back in her costume-sale special— frayed tuxedo jacket, long dress, glasses, and a pair of boots she'd found at a boutique near campus. "What's wrong with my clothes?"

"I find what you're wearing a little offensive."

Offensive? Lauren wondered what kind of comeback Winnie would have made to a comment like that. "Why?"

"If you don't know, I can't tell you." Marielle shook her head. "I don't know about you, Lauren. I just don't know."

Lauren tried not to smile.

Marielle put her hand to her forehead, as if she had a horrendous migraine. "I'm supposed to make you fit into this sisterhood, but you are just not giving me any help. I don't know how much further I'm supposed to go. I hope you're at least coming to the open house."

Lauren thought about walking through the

door with Dash in his bandanna and ink-stained clothes. "I'll be there."

"Good. Will you remember it's homecoming, not Halloween?"

"I'll try. Actually, I'm bringing someone."

Marielle's made-up eyes got huge. "You mean a guy?"

Lauren nodded.

"You're actually showing up with an escort? Well, hallelujah."

Lauren had to smile as she thought, *You can say that again!*

"Watch where you're going!"

Horns honked. Brakes squealed. KC narrowly missed running into a cyclist. Her legs flew and her arms pumped. When she bolted across a parking-lot exit without even looking at the cars, another driver yelled at her.

"You want to get killed?"

"Oh, just chill out," KC yelled back. *"This is important. I'm in a hurry."*

Even though KC loathed running, she didn't slow down. The campus security man had kept her on the phone forever! He'd made her borrow Lauren's note from the box again and read it to him. Then some art major had come down to the basement and KC had had to wait until he washed out what seemed like a hundred paintbrushes. And lastly she'd checked the Coleridge basement clock and realized that her grandfather's old timepiece had picked a terrible moment to start running slow.

So she hadn't even taken the time to drop off her jacket and cap. Her empty mail sack flapped over her shoulder as she puffed and ran. At least the bank was open late on Fridays. Still, she didn't have a second to spare.

She ran around one more corner, and the low cedar building finally came into view. The glass door swung open and a patron strolled out. Gasping for breath, KC ran faster. She was dizzy. Her throat was parched. She allowed herself one second to gulp from the drinking fountain, then raced to the bank's front door.

But just as KC put her arm out to push open the door, she saw a man locking the door from the inside. KC heard the bolt slide into place.

She flung herself against the glass. "Wait! Wait!" She pounded. "You can't close. I've got a paycheck to cash! Please! It'll take just a second."

The man looked at KC as if she were crazy.

"Let me in!" KC screamed. *"You have to let me in!"*

The man walked away. But when KC pounded again, he stopped in the middle of the lobby, took his key out again, and slowly came back toward the door.

KC heaved with relief. "Thank you, sir. Thank you," KC chanted. She waved and tried to express her eternal gratitude to him in gestures and signs.

Soon the bolt slid back and the door cracked opened. The man stuck out his head.

"Thank you so much. All I need to do is cash this. Thank you forever."

"Young lady, would you like to get yourself arrested?"

"What?"

"The bank is closed. Now stop this yelling and pounding, or I'm calling campus security."

KC stared at him.

The man locked the door again and walked away. As far as he was concerned, KC no longer existed. He didn't care that she was late because she'd been talking to campus security. He didn't care that she had to have that cash to pick up the shirts with Steven first thing Monday. He didn't care that her relationship with Steven, her reputation, and her pride depended on it!

KC took out her check and looked at the useless slip of paper. She put her mail cap over her face, sat down on the concrete, and began to cry.

Nine

"Would you pass the mustard?"

Winnie picked up the mustard in its yellow-and-red squeeze bottle. She watched with fascination as Matthew glopped a ribbon of it across his hot dog.

"I think this is the best mustard ever made for hot dogs," Matthew said.

"I agree."

"Hot dogs, mustard, Cheez Whiz, Coke. They all go together."

"How about corn dogs on a stick?"

"Too trendy." Matthew made a face and they both laughed.

The U of S stadium parking lot was packed

with tailgate picnickers, students celebrating the classic homecoming tradition of pregame picnicking out of their cars. The wind was still brisk, the sky partly cloudy. There was a wonderful excitement in the air. Everyone was wearing spirit buttons or red-and-white scarves. The band could be heard practicing inside the stadium and the Avalanche! banners flapped in the wind.

"This feels like a carnival," Winnie announced.

"It's like that scene in *Most Special Day*. Did you ever see that flick?"

"I don't think so."

"The way it moved from the state fair to the little family farm—what timing! It never lingered too long in one place. Never got sloppy. It was great."

"Was it a classic?" Winnie teased.

Matthew finished his hot dog and smiled.

So far, Winnie was having a good freshman homecoming. Matthew looked as handsome as she remembered in his black pants and turtleneck, his blond rattail curling down the back of his neck. He'd come by her dorm at exactly 1:45. Of course, Winnie had been running late, because she'd been goofing off in the hall, hoping that Josh might wander by. Matthew hadn't liked being kept waiting, because he had their whole afternoon planned out. Winnie had decided to flow with his plan. For once, she wasn't going to let her impulsiveness push things out of control.

"What now?" Winnie asked, finishing her hot dog and licking mustard off her palm. "I'm up for anything."

Matthew was loading the picnic supplies back into his car, an old red Mustang that was so immaculate you could eat off the tires. He'd brought a little Crockpot for the hot dogs, plus a hamper for the buns, condiments, and sodas. Now he was neatly repacking them all. Winnie made a move to toss in her dirty napkin, but he intercepted it and threw it in the trash.

"Sorry." Winnie looked around at their fellow picnickers. Plates of half-eaten chicken were scattered about. Someone shook up a soda can and sprayed his girlfriend with the fizz. Boom boxes boomed. People leaned against fenders and talked football. No one besides Matthew seemed in any kind of hurry.

Matthew locked up and turned back to her. "I thought we'd walk over to the band shell and catch the concert."

Winnie hung back. "We already have music," she said, pointing to a boom box. "Besides, we can hear the marching band playing inside the stadium."

"But there's a different band at the band shell."

Matthew took off, striding between the cars. "It's a local group, made up of doctors and dentists. They're doing John Philip Sousa. It should be great."

"If you say so." Winnie wove through the messy picnics as she tried to catch up. "Will we make it back for the beginning of the game?"

Matthew checked his watch. "If we keep on schedule."

Winnie broke into an easy lope. "Not that I mind missing the beginning of the game," she chattered. "I don't really understand the rules of football. All those downs and yard lines are totally confusing. I was a cheerleader one semester in high school along with my best friends, Faith and KC, but I kept doing the wrong cheers. I never cared, though, because I had such a good time."

"Cheerleading is classic," Matthew broke in. "Now I don't think football is such a great game, but it tells a lot about our culture. It's like television."

"I know what you mean."

"Like marching bands and frozen dinners. Like ranch-style houses, collie dogs, Hula-Hoops, and casseroles with crushed potato chips on top."

Winnie wasn't so sure she understood him. "Yes?"

"Ant farms, bowling, gas-guzzling cars, fast food. Do you know what I mean?"

"I think so."

"Sure you do." He crunched up his face, as if he were explaining something vitally important. "Like barbershop quartets, boardwalks, Slinkys, Tupperware, furniture with plastic covers over it."

"Like old Star Trek reruns?"

"Yes! That's it!" He slowed down and slung his arm around her. "You do know! A lot of people can't follow what I'm talking about half the time, but I knew when I saw you in film class that you were different. Special."

"You think so?" Winnie took a deep breath.

But Matthew kept talking. "I know we have to watch all these highbrow movies in class, but as far as I'm concerned, there's no better movie than *E.T.* Do you realize what it took for Spielberg to compose every sequence? It took genius. Pure genius. Every child in America should be required to memorize every frame in that flick, every shot."

"I don't know about *every* shot, *every* frame."

They left the parking lot and crossed the street, the carnival atmosphere fading away behind them. Matthew checked his watch again and led a sprint in the direction of the band shell.

Winnie ran easily. "I mean, I thought it was good when E.T. raided the refrigerator."

"Good?" Matthew sputtered. "Good? Spielberg is not good. Spielberg is genius. I'm going to do my film class term paper on him."

"I was going to do mine on Hitchcock."

"Everybody'll write about Hitchcock."

"That's okay." Winnie frowned. "I don't care about that."

Matthew slowed to a walk as the band shell came into view. A small crowd was gathered around it, and the band was playing off-key. Winnie had slowed down, too, until her feet came to a dead stop. Josh was standing to one side of the band shell, his leather jacket slung over his shoulder, a puzzled look on his handsome face.

"I can't believe how we're on the same wavelength," Matthew went on. He was walking right toward Josh!

Winnie tried to steer Matthew toward the back of the crowd, but Matthew wasn't paying much attention to her. And sure enough, Josh looked over. The next thing Winnie knew, Josh was smiling at her and waving.

"Somebody you know?" Matthew asked suspiciously, trying to make himself heard over the off-key brass.

Josh came over to join them. His eyes were full

of affection for Winnie and he sprang toward her to tousle her hair. Then he saw Matthew and took a step back.

"Josh, this is Matthew Kallender," Winnie said. "Um, Matthew, this is Josh Gaffey."

The two guys looked each other over.

"What is this?" Josh finally said, gesturing to the band. "I was just walking over to the game and I saw this going on." He laughed. "These guys are brutal. They redefine the words *tone deaf.*"

Matthew bristled. "This kind of band is not something everyone can appreciate."

"That's probably a good thing." Josh smiled. "I think I'll be able to appreciate the game, though. Maybe I'll see you over there." He took one more look at Winnie, then began to walk away.

Ignoring Josh, Matthew said to Winnie, "There's a parade happening downtown tomorrow, complete with square dancing. I thought we could go. Then we can catch a flick at the film society. I'll figure out the whole day."

"Yeah?" Winnie cringed as Josh turned back to wave and a doctor or dentist came forward for his off-key saxophone solo.

* * *

Where Lauren was sitting, it was quiet—too quiet. Only her nervous, shallow breathing, the purr of her BMW's perfectly tuned engine, and the distant car horns from the traffic backed up after the football game could be heard. She'd been parked in the loading zone for ten minutes, waiting for Dash to come out of the newspaper office.

"Nice car," said Dash as he swung open the passenger door and climbed in.

Lauren didn't want to acknowledge his reaction to her car. She didn't look at him. "Just put that stuff in the back," she said, realizing that she'd left some classical-music tapes on the seat. She hoped she hadn't left anything else for Dash to examine, such as the stupid color chart Marielle had given her. Or the note from the Progressive Students' Coalition, which she probably should have torn up and burned.

She turned to check the floor as Dash swiveled to throw her tapes onto the backseat. They almost knocked heads. Lauren gasped.

She stared at him.

He stared at her.

"Who's the split personality now?" she blurted. She was so stunned that for a second all the shyness was knocked out of her.

Dash's long hair was combed back, and the

bandanna was gone. His face was clean-shaven and for the first time she could see his angular cheeks and wide, expressive mouth. He had a nice face. A smart face. He wore a collarless striped shirt, pleated trousers, and high-tops. The only trace of his former image was the piece of gum being chomped between his teeth.

He pulled a pack of gum out of his pocket. "Want a piece?"

Lauren wondered if he was nervous, too, or was simply trying to stop smoking. "No, thanks."

"We won the game."

"What?"

"The football game. We won. Fourteen to six. I listened on the campus radio station."

Lauren fidgeted, then drove in silence. A hundred topics of conversation started and ended in her head as she wove through the campus and over to the street with all the sororities and fraternities. There was a lot of homecoming traffic, and the big, elaborate houses were lit up. Front doors had been propped open and the sidewalks were busy with Greek types, parents, and alums.

"There's a space," Dash pointed out.

Lauren whispered a thank-you and pulled into a spot that some frat guys were just leaving, right in front of the ODT house. Feeling awkward again, she got out of the car and walked with Dash. "The Tri Beta house is on the next block."

He looked up and down the street, hiking his shoulders as if he were a little self-conscious, too. Lauren couldn't help noticing that no matter how much Dash had cleaned up his act, he still was a far cry from the Greek types. They both were, since she was wearing another costume-sale special. She stole another glance at Dash, thought of the old woman from Bickford Lane, and told herself she was doing the right thing.

In another minute they were standing in front of the Tri Beta house, looking at the sparkling-clean windows, the white shingles, and the widow's walk on the roof. Pots of pink mums lined the walkway across the front lawn. Pledges and their well-heeled boyfriends were bunched up at the door.

Lauren and Dash slowly walked up the formal path. Dash tapped the Beta Beta Beta sign, and then they were both inside.

"Welcome, everyone. Welcome to our Tri Beta homecoming." Courtney Conner stood at the head of the reception line wearing a black velvet smock with a lace collar.

Lauren froze, waiting for Courtney to notice Dash.

With perfect poise, Courtney put out her hand

in greeting. She looked right at Dash but didn't react. "Hello."

"Hi." Lauren nervously pushed her glasses against her nose. She turned to Dash and almost stepped on his foot. "This is Dash Ramirez."

"Have we met?" Courtney asked him, all polite innocence.

Dash smiled as if he saw right through her. "Somehow I don't think we travel in the same circles."

"Dash is an assistant editor of the *Weekly Journal*," Lauren explained.

"Well, I'm very glad to meet you, Mr. Ramirez," responded Courtney, smooth as honey. "Welcome to our open house. Isn't it exciting that we won the game?"

Dash nodded.

"I don't suppose you're going to do an article on us," Courtney said, smiling. "What would you write about?"

"Who knows?" Dash rocked on his high-tops and began taking in the scene. "Anything's possible."

Lauren noticed a flicker of alarm in Courtney's eyes. She tensed, then reminded herself that this was going nearly the way she wanted it to.

"Well, do look around. I'm president of this sisterhood. If you need any information, you can always ask me." Courtney smiled and turned to the next guest.

Lauren led Dash down the reception line, where he shook hands with the housemother, more active members, and influential alums.

"That Courtney is slick," Dash muttered as they made their way away from the line. He wrung out his hand. "I haven't done that much greeting since my cousin Enrique's wedding."

They walked across the room to a long table where refreshments were being served. There were ribbons and doilies, enough flowers to perfume the whole house, and crepe-paper sashes draped from the ceiling. Lauren watched Dash stare at the fancy hors d'oeuvres, all so artistically arranged that it seemed a shame to eat them and ruin the design. It sure was a far cry from the newspaper potluck.

Nevertheless, Dash popped a turnover in his mouth. He stabbed a couple of pieces of crusty bread, wrinkled his nose at the fondue, and looked suspiciously at the foamy, melon-colored punch.

That was when Lauren spotted Marielle Danner and a few of the more bootlicking pledges coming toward them like a hungry wolf pack.

Marielle stopped, and the pledges fell in behind her. First she surveyed Lauren's outfit, a loose dress with big shoulder pads and a sparkly scarf of Winnie's. In contrast, Marielle wore a straight skirt, a boxy little jacket, diamond earrings, and a clunky charm bracelet. It seemed that every pledge wore a subtle variation of Marielle's tasteful outfit.

"Lauren," Marielle cooed, her hair swishing as she tossed her head, "I thought we talked about these new clothes of yours." She waved a finger and her charm bracelet clanked. "You look . . . interesting."

The other pledges tittered.

Something inside Lauren clenched. As much as she wanted to get kicked out of the Tri Betas, this brought back painful memories. During rush she had been set up as a joke "dream date." In reality, she'd been picked because she was the least dreamy girl in rush. The giggling pledges reminded her of how she'd been laughed at and humiliated.

Marielle homed in on Dash. "Who do we have here?"

"I'm Dash Ramirez," he said.

"Dash?" Marielle scoffed. "Is that a nickname?"

"Short for Dashiell. Like Dashiell Hammett. He was a writer. Ever hear of him?"

Marielle looked blank.

Dash didn't back down. "And who are you?"

"Dash, this is Marielle Danner."

Marielle didn't offer to shake Dash's hand. She stared as if she couldn't figure out what to make of him. He obviously wasn't a frat brat. But he obviously wasn't a nerd or a creep, either. Still, Marielle looked like she wanted to crush him between her little white teeth.

"So who are you, though?" Marielle insisted. "I mean, why should I care about who you are?"

Dash stiffened and Lauren knew he was ready to walk away.

"Dash is on the staff of the *Weekly Journal,*" Lauren stammered.

"Do you write stories, like Lauren does?"

Dash narrowed his dark eyes. "I'm a journalist."

Marielle kept sneering. "How do you get ideas for your articles?"

"I steal them," Dash told her, his face relaxing in an ironic smile.

"When do you write?"

"Late at night under a full moon."

The pledges giggled. Lauren smiled as well.

"Where?"

"Someplace dark, dank, and musty, preferably with a well-stocked refrigerator and a Chinese restaurant around the corner."

The pledges huddled closer.

"Do you write by hand or on a word processor?"

"I prefer to write in blood." Dash swaggered. "But when that's not available I use a 1947 Royal typewriter that weighs about forty-seven hundred pounds and takes six people to push down the keys."

Now the pledges started firing questions, too, with Marielle watching, her pretty face contorted in a frown.

"Is there anything you won't write about, Dash?"

"Boring stuff. Television. Yacht races. What goes on in places like this."

"This isn't boring."

"True, it's not as boring as a story on kitchen appliances or lawn fertilizers. Or"—Dash looked over the buffet table—"hors d'oeuvres."

To Lauren's amazement, the pledges laughed again. A couple of active members noticed the huddle and joined in.

"Okay," another pledge insisted, "what would you write if you were going to write about the Tri Beta house, though? I mean, honestly."

Dash looked at Lauren and rolled his eyes. "Well, first of all, I hardly ever write honestly. I prefer to write frankly, but sometimes I'll just settle for truthfully. Second, it seems to me I was asked that question when I came in. Any of you believe in déjà voodoo?"

"Déjà what?"

Lauren spun around to locate the new smooth, dusky voice. Courtney had joined the group and was staring at Dash, too. Lauren didn't know how long she'd been there. She wondered if Marielle had called Courtney over, if every word of Dash's was being recorded as evidence for Lauren's expulsion in a sorority supreme court. She hoped so.

As if she knew she'd been caught spying, Courtney launched into official business. "I just wanted to remind my girls that they're all due here tonight before they can go to any frat parties. We're going to announce who your secret sisters are." Courtney laughed and tapped Dash's shoulder. "Just us, of course. No press allowed."

Lauren was really suspect of Courtney's intentions now. Most pledges knew their sorority schedule better then their boyfriend's telephone number.

As if the pledges sensed Courtney's disapproval of Dash, they began to back away, whispering among themselves. A few turned for one last look at Dash, but soon they had all rejoined the rest of the Tri Beta homecoming crowd.

Lauren and Dash were alone again.

Lauren exhaled. She hadn't realized how tense she was. Her fists were clenched and her neck ached. "Can we get some air? I think that's about all I can take for a while."

"Me, too."

"I mean, we can come back," she backtracked. "But believe me, it's just going to be more of this all evening. It's not like the frat parties down the street. If you want to see wilder stuff, that's where you'll have to go. Those parties won't start until late, though. I don't know which frat house invited the Tri Betas. If you want, I can find out."

Dash took one last look around. "That's okay," he whispered. "I've got to meet Richard and Alison and make some posters for tomorrow. Some other time."

As they scooted together out the front door, Lauren wasn't sure which of them was in a bigger hurry to leave.

When the Tri Beta house was behind them, Dash began whistling "Who's Afraid of the Big Bad Wolf." Soon Lauren joined in. Then they were skipping and laughing. Lauren was even leaping and tapping at leaves hanging from trees. For once in her life, she felt light, giddy, even triumphant. When they passed the Kappa Kappa

Gamma house, Dash nodded at two sorority sisters.

"Fappa, Epsilon, Hamma," he said solemnly and nodded.

The girls glared at him and walked faster.

"I wish I could hear what all those girls are saying about me now," Lauren said. She stopped and put her face in her hands. "No, I don't," she admitted. "I really don't want to know."

Dash stopped whistling. "Who cares? It all seems pretty artificial. Not the stuff that makes the world go round."

"No," Lauren sighed. "Just the stuff that makes my mother's world go round."

Dash didn't ask her to explain. He started walking again, and soon they were standing by her car.

"Anyway . . ." she fumbled.

"Yeah, well . . ." Dash said, suddenly at a loss for words, too.

They stood on the sidewalk watching a frat pack walk by, reviewing the details of the game. Finally Lauren spoke up again. "Do you live in the dorms?"

"I live off campus. I can walk."

"You sure you don't want a ride?"

"Nah. I'm just going home to change and then I'm heading over to Richard and Alison's. It's not far. We have a lot to do to get ready for tomorrow."

"Can I help?"

Dash shrugged. "You could, but I think it would make Alison too paranoid if you showed up. Better just join us tomorrow. You clear on how it's all going to work?"

"I think so." Lauren lingered. "Thanks for coming with me to this."

"Hey, don't thank me. You were the one taking a chance, letting a heathen like me in a place like that. It took some guts."

"Not really."

"Oh, yeah." He stuck his hands in his pockets and looked at the ground. "From what I've heard, they tie you up and make you chant secret sorority songs just for looking at guys like me."

Looking at him? Lauren felt breathless. Had she been *looking* at him? Was it at all possible that Dash saw her in that way? Since she had next to no experience with guys, she really didn't know.

"Anyway," she said. "I don't care what they do. I want to quit soon, anyway."

"Yeah?" Lightly, almost imperceptibly, he reached over and touched her shoulder. His dark eyes became softer. "I knew there was something I liked about you."

"Really?"

He shrugged. "Sure."

Lauren told herself not to get carried away. This was hardly a romantic outing. Dash had just been doing research to satisfy some journalistic curiosity. No matter what he said about her "looking" at him, there was no more to it than that. And yet, Lauren felt like she was floating a few inches above the sidewalk.

A little embarrassed, Dash started to walk away. "Okay. Well. See you tomorrow."

"See you then."

He waved. "Tomorrow we make things change."

"Good-bye."

Lauren opened the door to her car and realized that she couldn't wait for things to change. She was suddenly ready for her entire life to be transformed.

Ten

· · · · · · · · · · · · · ·

"*H*ow do I look?" KC asked.

She was standing in the doorway of Faith and Lauren's room. Her hair was held back by little combs. She wore a black sweater and a knife-pleated skirt.

"Beautiful," Faith assured her. She was sitting on her bed, wearing a simple denim jumper and a soft cotton sweater. "You always look beautiful, but tonight I'm in such a good mood that everything and everyone looks beautiful."

Winnie, who was sweaty in her neon running tights, waved her hands. "Look out, Christopher! After facing the world with Faith Crowley on your arm tonight, life may never be the same."

KC paced from the mirror to the doorway and back again, while Lauren turned away.

"You look nice," Lauren muttered.

"Gee, thanks," KC shot back.

Faith and Winnie exchanged glances. Despite their good cheer, the tension between KC and Lauren was so thick Faith felt she could choke on it. Faith had invited KC to get ready in her room only because KC was suddenly acting like such a mental case. Faith had assumed that it would be just the three of them, since Lauren was supposed to have gone back to her sorority house.

"KC, you look a little conservative for my taste," Winnie chattered, sprawling on the floor and stretching. "But you do look impressive. If I were Steven's father, I'd buy a used car from you any day."

KC didn't laugh.

Lauren stared at her computer screen.

"Are you okay, KC?" Faith asked.

KC bit a fingernail.

"It's only Steven's father, you know," Winnie reminded her, "not the president of the United States."

"I know."

"You're not even that serious about Steven. Are you?"

KC fretted. "Sometimes I like him. Sometimes I hate him. But there's a lot more to it than that. I just wish I'd never said I'd go to dinner before this whole dumb soccer-shirt thing is over and done!" She put her hands to her face. "Never mind. I'm sorry. You don't understand."

"Then explain it to us," Winnie said.

KC glanced at Lauren, frowned, then checked her skirt. "Are you sure this looks okay?"

"Yes!" Faith and Winnie said at the same time.

"All right. I'm going back to my dorm. That's where Steven is picking me up."

"Have a good time," Faith called.

"Just relax. Don't chew your ice," yelled Winnie. "If anything momentous happens, come to my room later and wake me up."

"Me, too," added Faith.

As soon as KC's footsteps had faded away, Winnie said, "KC is sure freaked-out all of a sudden. Did something happen yesterday?"

"Not that I know of."

Lauren shut off her computer and turned on her CD player. For half a CD, Winnie did sit-ups while Lauren stewed and Faith counted the songs, her heart thunking to the beat as every chorus went by. Christopher was late.

Finally Lauren turned down the music. "It's probably just being near me."

"What?"

"The way KC is acting. I think it's because of me. She hates me so much."

"She doesn't hate you," soothed Faith. She got up and checked the clock. She opened her window and looked out over the dark green, which was lit by the occasional lamppost. She saw dressed-up couples crisscrossing the concrete paths, waving U of S pennants and laughing. Crisp mountain air floated in. She told herself that Christopher must have gotten bogged down with some kind of fraternity business.

Winnie folded herself into a yoga contortion and peeked up at Lauren. "I thought you had to go back to the sorority. Isn't there some secret-sister weirdness happening?"

Lauren nodded. "I decided not to go."

"Good for you." Winnie applauded.

"I thought I'd get some homework done. I have a big day tomorrow." Lauren looked out the window, too, and took a nervous breath.

"Are you seeing that newspaper guy again?" Winnie gasped. "Did you tell Faith about your date?"

Lauren sighed. "It was hardly a real date."

"Sorry. I'm no expert on that subject." Winnie

threw herself back on the floor and kicked her legs. "You know, I came home from the game, and there was a note on my door from Josh saying he'd stopped by on the spur of the moment. He must have left that note before the game because I ran into him with Matthew. Now Josh probably thinks I'm not interested." She let out a little scream. "Oh well. Matthew may be overly into planning, but I think my life needs more of that. I think we're doing five different classic activities tomorrow, from eating breakfast at Denny's to watching them take apart the floats from the homecoming parade. And I plan to have a fabulous time."

Winnie turned on Lauren's TV. The three of them sat on Faith's bed and watched for a while. Again, as each scene, each commercial flickered past, Faith began to worry. Her throat became dry and her pulse sped up. Christopher was almost forty-five minutes late!

They watched a Jell-O commercial, a public-service announcement, and a preview for a new show. When the theme song for the next sitcom came on, Faith had to face the fact that another half-hour had passed. She checked the window again, held back her tears, and began to pace.

When she was near the door she saw Kimberly, the dancer from next door, striding toward her, waving and smiling. Kimberly was dressed up, too, and was accompanied by a tall flute player who lived downstairs.

"Faith," Kimberly called, "hall phone for you!"

"For me?" Faith was momentarily paralyzed.

"Yes. It's a guy."

With Lauren and Winnie staring, Faith bolted down the hall. She grabbed the telephone receiver as if it were her lifeline. "Hello?"

It took a while for someone to answer. In those few moments Faith worried that something horrible had happened.

At last Christopher said, "Faith?" He sounded tired.

"Christopher, where are you? Why aren't you here? What happened?"

"I'm sorry." There was a pause, filled by some crackly static and a few mushy, far-off-sounding voices.

"Where are you?"

"Uh, downtown," he finally said. "I'm still working on this news shoot for the TV station. I couldn't call you before this. I've been here all day."

Faith felt her heart drop. "When will you be done?"

"I don't know. I think we'd better just cancel for tonight. I'm sorry, Faith. I really am."

"But it's homecoming." Faith couldn't believe what was flashing through her mind. She'd always been a trusting person, but suddenly all she could think was that Christopher was lying to her. She wondered if he'd ever really told Suzanna not to come. What if he was calling from his frat house, with Suzanna waiting for him in his room?

"What about tomorrow? Can we do something then?" Faith sensed that she was being clingy, even desperate. But she wanted to know where things stood. And she wanted to know soon, before their relationship went any further.

"Tomorrow?"

"Maybe we can do something else at your house. I thought this whole weekend was one big party on Greek row." It was vital to her that they do something public, surrounded by his friends and his real life.

"I have to work at the TV station tomorrow, too."

"The whole day?"

Another pause followed. "The whole day."

Faith wasn't sure what to say next. She didn't know whether this was the end or merely a small step backward. She didn't know whether she should back out right then or wait and see.

"Please don't be angry, Faith. You know how

important this internship is to me. I'm sure in a few weeks it'll get better. I'll talk to you soon."

"When? Where?"

"Don't worry," he said. "I'll find you. I've got to go back to work now. I'm sorry. 'Bye."

Faith held the phone while the dial tone buzzed at her. All her excitement had curdled inside her, making her feel heavy and sick. For a moment she couldn't walk, so she leaned against the wall.

What will happen now? she wondered. There were no more rehearsals, no more opening nights. Would she just wait for Christopher to pop out of the sky and surprise her whenever he felt like it? Would she wait patiently, putting the rest of her emotional life on hold while he waited to introduce her to his friends?

All Faith knew was, she couldn't handle this alone. She began to trudge slowly back to her room. She'd had enough secrecy for a lifetime and she was glad that Winnie was there.

But before she reached her door, she remembered Lauren. Faith couldn't talk about Christopher in front of her. She'd seen Lauren cringe earlier when Winnie had just mentioned Christopher's name. And why shouldn't Lauren feel awful? She'd been set up during rush as Christopher's joke "dream date," and although it hadn't been Christopher's fault, Faith couldn't blame Lauren for never wanting to hear his name again.

Faith took a quick detour into the bathroom, where she splashed cold water on her face and hands. She waited until she felt like herself again, then went back to her room.

Lauren was back at her computer and Winnie was reading Faith's Western Civ text. As soon as Faith came in, Winnie sprang up, looking first curious, then alarmed.

"It was just my little sister on the phone," Faith lied. "I'm going to go out and walk over to that party. Win, why don't you walk with me?"

Recognizing Faith's distress, Winnie quickly joined her. Lauren continued to type away, pausing only to wave and say goodnight.

As soon as they were out the lobby door, Faith grabbed Winnie's arm, rested her head on her shoulder and said, "Am I glad you're here. That was Christopher on the phone. He stood me up."

When KC had imagined Steven Garth's father, she'd thought of a silver-haired corporate oilman, elegant and immaculately dressed. She'd imagined a voice as refined as Lauren's, only razor-sharp, aggressive, and quick. She'd expected him to dote on his handsome, clever son while she sat quietly and tried not to slurp her soup.

But Mr. Garth wasn't like that at all. Instead, he was overweight and balding. He smoked cigars. He talked in a loud, twangy voice, wore a leisure suit, and carried a cowboy hat. And instead of focusing on Steven, he seemed much more interested in KC.

"So tell me more about this business project, young woman," Mr. Garth commanded as he sawed at his well-done T-bone steak. The restaurant was a bustling steak joint called the Sacred Cow. It had gathered white curtains and little green lamps on the walls. Like Steven's father, it was robust, friendly, and expensive-looking.

"Well, I got the idea from seeing the dorm teams practicing. I noticed that they didn't have uniforms. And I know how excited and competitive people get about intramural sports—even though they pretend they're playing just for fun."

Mr. Garth laughed. "Good observation. Now Steven thinks people do everything just for fun. Don't you, son?"

Steven stopped eating. Ever since they'd joined his father, he'd seemed angry, almost sullen. His clothes looked intentionally rumpled.

KC cut into her steak and continued, "So I thought they'd want some way to identify their teams. See, we were required to do this project for our business class and I didn't want to do something as mundane as a book report."

"It's always better to cut your own path," Mr. Garth said.

"Actually, I've been working on this, too, Dad," Steven interrupted. "Believe it or not, I don't just sit around in class staring at my watch."

"Is that so?" Mr. Garth threw his son the slightest glance, then turned his attention back to KC.

KC took a big breath. "And I already knew a little bit about working in a small business, so I thought buying soccer shirts from a supplier downtown and selling them to the teams might be a good idea."

"Sounds good to me."

"KC knows about small businesses because her parents own one," explained Steven, leaning over his untouched plate. "A very small business."

KC tried to laugh while flashing Steven an angry look. She didn't know why he was suddenly bringing up something that he knew would embarrass her.

"What kind of business?" asked Mr. Garth.

"What?"

"Your family, KC. What kind of business are they in?"

"Food service," said KC.

"A health-food joint," Steven corrected. "It's a real return-to-the-sixties thing." He speared a chunk of steak with his fork. "If you tried to order one of these there, they'd have you arrested."

Mr. Garth ignored him. "The restaurant business is tough."

"Yes," said KC, gritting her teeth. For some reason, Steven was really bent on humiliating her. She tried to ignore him and focus solely on his dad. "It is. So's the oil business. Right?"

Mr. Garth winked at her. "Smart girl."

"That's right, Dad," Steven intruded again. "Believe it or not, smart girls actually go on dates with me."

"Do they?" Mr. Garth responded blandly.

For a while KC and Mr. Garth ate, while Steven shook his head and watched the waiters. KC tried to contain her anger. She was beginning to suspect that this dinner was about something more than simply meeting Steven's father.

"So Monday you deliver your shirts and see what kind of profit you've made. Is that right?" Mr. Garth finished his steak and ordered a gooey desert.

KC tried not to choke, thinking about the

cash she didn't have and what would happen on Monday. "We'll see. But I guess the most important thing is how much we've learned. Right, Steven?"

Mr. Garth didn't wait for a response. "The important thing is what you do! I don't know how much you can learn in a classroom, anyway. I was out in the oil fields by the time I was thirteen. I came from nothing, and built my business myself." He winked at KC. "I bet you understand that. I can tell already that you've got guts, drive —what it takes to get ahead in this world."

"KC does understand that," Steven responded angrily. "She comes from some small town a few hours away from here. It's probably pretty close to nothing."

KC put down her knife and fork. Her appetite was gone. Steven was never easy to read, but she was beginning to understand what was going on. This was Steven's form of rebellion, as Winnie's mother would say. Steven wanted to annoy his father by showing him the lowlife girl he was seeing. Maybe that had been the cause of Steven's attraction to her from the very start.

At least KC didn't have to endure any more insults from Steven, because just then the waiter set a telephone on the table. She and Steven sat quietly, making silent, furious eye contact while his father took business calls.

After that, Mr. Garth didn't seem to be interested even in KC. They rushed through dessert so he could get back to his hotel and finish his business dealings.

After thanking Mr. Garth, KC climbed back into Steven's black Corvette. She sat facing the window, as far away from Steven as possible. Her heart was pounding and her anger burned inside her. For a long time Steven drove through the damp, cold night without speaking. When they pulled into the dorm parking lot, he finally said. "Look, Angeletti, I'm sorry. It's complicated. I'll explain it to you someday."

"You don't need to explain anything. Why didn't you just treat me like the waitress?" KC accused. "You could have asked me to take away your dirty dishes and refill your water glass."

Steven turned to her. His face looked sad and strained. He rubbed his hand over his forehead as if he were trying to straighten out his thoughts. "That's not it."

"It isn't? Why didn't you just come right out and tell him I'm a phony? Because it's true. I'm no corporate baby. My parents aren't business whizzes."

"What are you talking about, my little angel?"

KC blew up. "I'm no angel, Steven. And I'm not anyone's little anything. Why didn't you just tell him I'm a lowlife?"

"Why would I tell him that?"

"Because I am! I'm just a lowlife and a thief!"

Steven's mouth fell open. "KC, I'm sorry about how I acted. But I don't know what you're talking about."

KC almost started to laugh. Why had she worked so hard to hide her mistake? Steven would probably like her better for it. "You're going to find out on Monday, so I might as well tell you now. I borrowed—no, I *stole* three hundred dollars from our Soccer, Inc. account to pay off my stupid credit card. Why don't you tell that to your father, if you really want to impress him with how low you've stooped?"

Steven's face went white. For once there was no trace of mockery in his expression. "You took money from our business account?"

KC bit back tears. "Yes."

"If you needed money, Angeletti, why didn't you just ask me? That's the one thing my father's always willing to give."

"Look, if you want to show your father you think he's a jerk, do it with some other girl. Maybe my parents aren't heads of some huge corporation. Maybe I do come from a little hick town. But that's who I am. And you know what? Maybe I should be proud of it instead of trying to be the same kind of jerk as you."

"KC—"

The last thing KC saw was the terrible sadness in Steven's eyes. After that she was running across the green to look for Faith and Winnie.

Eleven

Lauren was freezing cold, standing with Dash and the others in Northwest Park. Her teeth chattered and her hands stung, but for once in her sheltered life, she felt that nothing could stand in her way.

"Are we all ready?" demanded Alison Argonbright in a fierce whisper.

"Is everyone clear on the plans from here?" seconded Richard Levine, nervously pulling on his beard.

Lauren looked at Dash.

Dash smiled at her. "You okay?" he asked.

"I think so."

Two dozen other members of the Progressive

Students' Coalition took deep, frosty breaths. They were hidden by the dark.

"Does everyone have their signs?" Richard commanded.

Nods.

"How about the masks?"

Nods again.

"Tape recorder?"

"Got it."

"Are you all clear on how to use the fake blood?"

Lauren and the others patted the packets of red paint stowed in their shirt pockets.

"Ready."

"Let's go."

"Don't be overeager," Alison cautioned them while Richard checked his watch. "We start moving in exactly four minutes. That's when Jake Dovorsky is going to unlock the kitchen door."

The guerrilla protest plan was worthy of Faith and her drama friends. Jake, a Coalition member who worked in the President's Hall kitchen, was sneaking them in through the delivery entrance. From there they would storm the reception room, chanting slogans and enacting scenes of people being thrown out of their homes. After that, Alison would stage a mock death, during which each of them would spatter her with fake blood. They even had a recording of old Hilda Markman's words, which they were going to play at full volume over the mayhem and the chants.

"Does anybody know if the TV crew is here?" Dash asked. He was back in normal Dash clothes, a bandanna and patched jeans. Dark camouflage paint was smeared on his face.

"They plan to be here." Richard quickly stretched his legs, as if preparing for a sprint. "They're going to film the regents and all the fat cats that give money to this university."

"So unless there's a big fire somewhere else tonight," Alison added, "or a four-car accident, those cameras should be ready."

"Good," Lauren said, catching Dash's eye again.

He touched her shoulder.

Then everyone began to collect their things and look out toward President's Hall, which was on the other side of the park, lit up like some kind of spaceship. They could see the occasional pair of car headlights swerving into the parking lot.

Dash held up his hands, then stepped forward to get everyone's attention. "Remember, we're doing this for those news cameras. The regents and their rich buddies won't change a thing unless this whole state knows about the people who live on Bickford Lane. We want to create so much publicity and so much pressure that the regents will have to back down and leave those houses alone."

Coalition member after coalition member nodded in agreement.

Alison checked her watch. She took off her Ben Franklin glasses and pulled on a stocking cap. "Okay," she breathed. "It's time. Everybody get in formation."

They lined up to march across the park. Lauren took her place alongside Dash. She held her placard and checked her packet of blood. When she looked up again, she saw Alison staring at her.

"Scared?" Alison asked.

For about the first time in her life, Lauren *didn't* feel scared. She knew that this was no sorority bash. She knew this was an act that would have consequences. But that only made her feel more brave. "I'm okay."

Alison looked surprised. "Good luck." Then she left Lauren and took her place again at the head of the group.

Richard checked his watch, counted off the last seconds, then ordered them forward with one strong, silent wave.

A bolt of electricity shot through Lauren. She

marched behind Alison, aware the whole time of Dash at her side. With each step she felt stronger, more righteous, and freer. Thoughts of her mother faded into the background. Marielle and the Tri Betas didn't matter. All that Lauren could think about now was Hilda Markman and the other people whose homes she was trying to save.

They reached the street that rimmed the park. President's Hall was on the other side, giving off a murmur of polite chatter. They could see the big chandelier through the side picture window and the people in tuxes and furs getting out of fancy cars and strolling in the front door.

Alison stretched out her arms and they all waited for a lull in the traffic. Then she gave a sudden, low grunt. Richard waved them on again, and they all ran together, like commandos, across the street.

As Lauren leapt up onto the opposite curb, Dash took her hand. He held it hard, conveying as much strength and conviction as she herself felt right then. She paused for one brief moment to look at his face. His dark eyes were filled with passion. There was the tiniest smile on his face, but it wasn't a smile of amusement. It was an expression of pride and the knowledge that they were doing the right thing.

.

Lauren took a deep, stirring breath. She raised her head and held up her placard, ready to face anything that could possibly happen. But then with the moonlight glowing and the adrenalin flowing wildly, her courage went dead and her mind blanked.

Something had gone wrong.

"What's going on?" Dash whispered.

"Who are those people?" Lauren asked.

A dark line of people was marching toward them. They were far enough off so that at first Lauren couldn't make out who they were. She hoped it might just be a group of alumni out for a walk. But soon she could see that the line was straight, the formation purposeful—just as purposeful as the coalition's.

Alison and Richard seemed to panic. "Where did they come from?"

"How did they know we'd be here?"

"Oh my God."

"Oh no."

Lauren began to tremble, too, when she noticed that the people were in uniform. As they stomped closer, she saw their riot helmets and threatening wooden sticks.

"Police!"

"Campus security."

"How did they know we were coming?"

"It's like they're waiting for us," Dash swore.

"Freeze, all of you," the head officer ordered. The other officers stood behind him, forming a barricade between the coalition members and the building.

Lauren and the others froze, with Alison facing the officer.

"You have no right to stop us!" Alison exploded. "We've just come to give a message. We're just using our freedom of speech."

"Not in this building, you're not," the officer threatened. "This is a private affair. No uninvited guests allowed."

"We have the right of assembly!" yelled Richard.

"You can assemble all you want," the officer barked back. "You just can't assemble in President's Hall, unless you want to spend the night in jail."

Alison and Richard looked at each other.

Dash turned away in disgust.

"How did they know we were coming?" Lauren asked Alison as they began to shuffle back across the street.

Alison refused to answer as they retreated into the dark of Northwest Park and the TV news crew filed into President's Hall.

* * *

"There isn't enough light in here."

"Too bad we can't shoot off the reflection of some of those diamonds. Jeez, I've never seen so many rocks in one place."

"Well, get them on film. Maybe we can make this into a fashion segment. Otherwise nobody's going to watch this regents' reception and stay awake. Where's that intern? Where's Chris Hammond?"

Christopher made his way over to the TV news producer. The regents and their VIP guests were milling around, looking bored in their black ties and jewels, waiting for the president of the university and the governor to arrive. Meanwhile, the TV crew had to find a way to make the reception look exciting for the eleven o'clock news. The producers were nervous. The cameraperson was on edge. And Christopher, Mr.-On-Top-of-It-BMOC, felt as inept and jumpy as a freshman. This was ten times worse then opening a show or speaking before the Interfraternity Council. All his life he'd wanted to work in TV, but now he couldn't do anything right.

Christopher pulled himself out of his daze. "Here I am, sir. What do you need?"

"Chris, can you run out and get another cable from the van?"

"Right away." Christopher hesitated a split second, and his mind wandered. Here he was, finally doing the job he'd always dreamed of, and all he could think about was his crazy personal life. Faith. Suzanna. Suzanna. Faith. They bounced back and forth in his head like the ball at a tennis match. He wasn't used to having things this complicated.

How was he supposed to have known that despite his casual request that Suzanna stay away, she would show up the night before for his frat party? Maybe he hadn't come right out and told her, *don't come, I'm seeing someone else.* But he'd hinted that he was busy and tired and she'd be better off staying home. He wasn't used to having to lie, as he'd done the previous night to Faith. He was used to girls who made him feel competent and powerful, not one whose image stayed in his head, making him so crazy that he couldn't work.

Trying to get his mind off Faith and Suzanna, Christopher took in the reception. People were shaking hands and staring at the floor, as if they couldn't wait to get this over with and do something fun. No wonder the producers were uptight. The footage was going to look as dull as dirt. There was nothing to film except people eating hors d'oeuvres.

Then Christopher heard someone clear his

throat. He looked up and realized he was still standing next to the producer.

"Did I ask you to go get me some cable or not?" the producer asked angrily.

"Oh. Yes, sir, you did. I'm sorry."

"Don't be sorry, Hammond. Just go get it."

Christopher nodded, trying to keep his concentration, and ran off in the direction where he thought he would find the cable.

"All right, so I made a mistake. I thought he was Mr. Right, and he turned out to be a dweeb."

"What, Winnie?"

"A dweeb, KC. A bore. Matthew. Mr. Real Date from my film class. Oh well, it's not the first time I've been wrong about some guy. And somehow I don't think it's going to be the last."

"That's nice," Faith mumbled.

"No, Faith, it wasn't nice. It was torture. I can't believe I spent the whole day with him. I should have known after yesterday that he was the epitome of dweebiness. I can't believe I gave up the chance of running into Josh so I could do the classic campus tour with Matthew the Dweeb. I would even have had a better time studying, or doing my laundry." Winnie waited for a response. When none came, she huffed and threw up her hands. "Is either of you listening to me?"

"Didn't you say something about dweebiness?" mumbled Faith.

KC signaled for quiet.

"Yeah, yeah," Winnie sighed. "I know, KC, your dorm has a twenty-four-hour quiet rule. But if we're going to start hanging out here we may have to bend the rules a little."

Since KC's traumatic dinner with Steven and his father the previous night, Faith and Winnie had been offering moral support by hanging around KC's single room in Langston Hall, the girls-only study dorm. Still, KC hadn't cheered up. She was lying, lumplike, on her bed while Faith stared blankly out the window. Unlike Faith's and Winnie's dorm rooms, KC's room was undecorated. There were no old photos or reminders of home—only the wooden eaves, the orders for her soccer shirt business and a stack of textbooks.

"So have you two been this exciting all day?" Winnie leaned back against the door, then slid down until she plopped onto the floor. "Haven't you moved all day? I seem to recall that when I left you after breakfast you were both in these exact same positions."

"I read the Sunday paper," said KC.

"We did some homework," Faith muttered.

"Sounds great," Winnie came back sarcastically. "Sounds like the most exciting freshman Sunday on record."

Faith finally stood up, stretching in her overalls and Western Drama Festival T-shirt. Her hair was in a messy braid. "I'm sorry, Win. I just keep thinking about Christopher, wondering why he really broke off our date and what's going to happen now that the play is over."

"Oh."

"When Brooks and I were together," Faith reasoned, "maybe it wasn't very exciting, but at least I knew where things stood. I can't handle not knowing what's going on."

"I think I'd rather not know what was going on than be so sure of everything that's happening," said KC, curling up in a ball. "Unfortunately, I know exactly why Steven treated me the way he did and just how he was using me to irritate his father. It was so obvious." She moaned. "I don't know why I didn't just march out of the restaurant as soon as he opened his mouth."

Faith stared and sighed, while KC pulled her blanket over her legs.

Winnie shook her hands, making her bracelets jangle. "No offense, you guys, but you two are not exactly thrilling company today. Maybe I underestimated Matthew. Compared to you, he's downright fascinating. Maybe hot dogs, Cheez Whiz, and classic movies aren't so bad after all." Winnie finally resorted to grabbing Faith's foot and pretending to bite her ankle. Then she got up, jumped on KC, and began to tickle her.

"Okay, okay!" KC cried. "I give up!"

"I'm sorry we're so wasted," added Faith, taking her eyes off the window. "Cheer us up. Tell us what you and Matthew did today."

"That may not cheer you up, but I hope it'll at least make you laugh." Winnie sat next to KC, then patted the bed until Faith sat on her other side. "Okay. We went to brunch at Denny's, where we had to order the classic Pigs in a Blanket. Then we hurried to the homecoming parade, which we had to leave at exactly one-ten so we could see a matinee of *Pillow Talk,* a movie Matthew was seeing for the seventeenth time—I kid you not. At least he didn't talk until the end. Then we walked all over campus looking for the place where they take apart the homecoming-parade floats. We never saw the floats, but we did see the dorm soccer teams working out. We saw some people doing a science experiment at Mill Pond. We saw the film crew from the TV news down by that regents' reception—"

Faith gasped.

Winnie kept right on talking. "Matthew does win a prize as the first guy who wouldn't let me get a word in edgewise. By the end of today I'd stopped even trying to talk. Can you imagine? Me, silent?"

Faith grabbed her wrist. "Winnie."

"Finally Matthew took me back to my dorm, and kissed me good-bye while I thought about how much I missed Josh and stood there like a potted plant. At least Matthew must have figured out that I don't like him. I won't have to worry about getting dumped this time. I'm sure he won't be back for more."

"Winnie!"

"What?"

Faith stood up. There was a wild look in her eyes. "You saw the local TV-news crew on campus?"

"Huh? Oh. Yes."

"When?"

"Just now. Just before I came over here. They were starting to set up before going into President's Hall. I guess there's some reception going on."

Faith was already pulling on her fringed suede jacket. She grabbed Winnie, then pulled KC up from her bed.

"What are you doing?"

"Are you nuts, Faith? What's going on?"

Faith turned back to them and whispered desperately, "If Christopher is with that TV-news crew, then I'll know he really had to work today and he was telling me the truth. And if he isn't, then I'll know he's a liar. I have to go over to President's Hall and find out for myself."

"We'll go with you," KC offered.

"If you're sure you really want to know," Winnie warned.

"Let's go," Faith urged as they left KC's single room and hurried down the stairs.

Twelve

. . . .

"**S**omebody ratted."

"Alison, why do you think that?"

"They were waiting for us. The cops were obviously standing there waiting for us to walk up to them. Someone had to have told them exactly what we were planning to do."

Lauren, Dash, and the other coalition members sat in a circle on an unlit tennis court in Northwest Park. Moonlight filtered through the net. The breeze shook the chain-link fence, and the gate clinked. It made Lauren think of country-club vacations with her parents, while at the same time it reminded her of TV shows about outlaws on the run.

"What do we do now?" asked Dash in a muted voice. His cigarette glowed in the dark night. Posters were scattered about him, as well as masks, jackets, packets of fake blood, and the boom box containing Hilda Markman's heart-rending tape.

"We don't do anything." Richard sagged in defeat. "There's no way we'll get into that building now, unless we're prepared to fight with the cops."

"Get real."

"No way."

"Let's just go home."

Lauren slowly raised her hand, as if she were sitting politely in English lit class. Alison and Richard ignored her. They both made moves to collect their belongings, as if the group was ready to break up.

Dash stopped them. "What, Lauren?"

"Well . . ."

He shushed the others. "What do you want to say?"

Lauren stood up and cleared her throat. "I was just thinking," she began, her voice barely squeaking out. "We're here and we're all ready. There must be something else we can do besides just quit. Even if we fail, we should at least try and get our message across. We've got to do something that might help those people on Bickford Lane."

"And just what do you have in mind?" Alison stood up, too, her hands on her hips as if she were facing off with Lauren.

Not looking at Alison, Lauren continued. She wasn't sure where her courage was coming from. She only knew that if she backed down now, she might never feel brave again. "I'm not sure. But the police only said we couldn't go into President's Hall. Maybe, we could hold our demonstration in the parking lot or right across the street in the park."

"That'll do a lot of good," Alison spat back. "No one will see us." She glared at Lauren, then at Dash.

"Alison," Dash objected, "lighten up. What Lauren says makes sense. Just because it's not your idea doesn't mean it isn't worth listening to."

"That's not my objection," Alison stated angrily.

Richard and the rest of the coalition members stared up at them in the moonlight. Lauren stayed standing, although her knees had begun to shake. Alison's glare burned through her.

"Well, then, think about what Lauren just said," Dash insisted. "Maybe she's right. So what if our plans didn't work out? Maybe there's another way. We can't just give up."

"Oh yes we can," Alison scoffed. "What makes you think that anything else we try tonight will stand a chance of getting seen by anyone? It's obvious to me, and it should be to you, that there's an informer in this group. That's why the police were waiting. And that's why anything else we try tonight will get stopped, too. We might as well go home."

The rest of the coalition members looked up with wide eyes.

Dash stomped out his cigarette. "What are you talking about?"

"I'm talking about your friend," Alison accused. She pointed at Lauren.

"Me?" Lauren felt a clutch in her throat. With all her new-found strength, she held back tears. "Why would I be an informer?"

"Someone told the police about our plans. And isn't it funny that you're the only one who still wants to go ahead with this?" Alison took in the whole group, as if she were making a speech to a jury. "You know, I do research on any new people who want to work with the coalition— and I know who you are, Lauren Turnbell-Smythe." She walked toward Lauren, pointing a finger. "I know that you're a sorority girl and that your parents are as rich as those pig regents. Now why would someone like that want to join our cause?"

"Because I believe in what you're trying to do."

"Don't give me that."

Lauren looked at Dash. There was a trace of doubt in his eyes, too.

Richard addressed Dash. "Somebody snitched. Or else somebody was careless with their written message and let it fall into the wrong hands—which is just as bad. Lauren's the only new person here. And you have to admit that her background is pretty suspicious. If it wasn't Lauren, who do you think it was?"

Everyone looked at the person next to them with a little less comfort and camaraderie than they'd shown a moment before. Lauren knew they had to find a scapegoat. And they were all deciding that she was the villain.

In that moment every horrible freshman memory came rushing back to Lauren: KC's betrayal, Marielle's snobbishness, and being set up as Christopher Hammond's "dream date." Lauren's whole body trembled and she wanted to sink into the earth.

"Why did you do it, Lauren?" one coalition member said accusingly.

"What are you, a spy for the regents?"

"Go back to your sorority."

"You'd better not show your face around any of us again."

Dash took a step forward and Lauren sensed that he was going to defend her. But she couldn't sit back and let Dash speak for her.

For once in her life, Lauren had to do something brave, even reckless. "Look, what if I walk back over to the hall and see if the police are still there?" Lauren offered. "Maybe I can sneak into the kitchen, contact Jake, and see if we can make another plan."

"Go home, sorority girl," barked a coalition member.

"We don't need you doing anything for us."

"Go back to Sorority Row," they began to chant.

"Hey!" Dash suddenly exploded. "What is going on here? Since when do we condemn people without evidence? I thought we stood for the opposite of all that. Give Lauren a chance!"

Silence hovered over the tennis court. The coalition members would no longer look at one another.

"Go ahead, Lauren Turnbell-Smythe," Alison finally dared her. "But just remember: you can't trick us and get away with it. We'll find out the truth about every move you make."

"I have nothing to hide," Lauren said. She met Dash's dark, trusting eyes one more time before taking off into the night, heading for President's Hall.

"He's right there, go talk to him."

"Winnie, I don't want Christopher to think I came here to spy on him."

"But that's exactly what you did, Faith. At least go and say hello. KC and I will go with you if you want."

"Speak for yourself, Win," whispered KC. "I'm not getting any closer to that reception hall. I think Steven's father is inside. And I don't want to see him again as long as I live."

"Oh, well." Winnie shrugged. "I guess we're not dressed for a VIP reception, anyway." She laughed at Faith's overalls, her own tights and satin boxers, and KC's blazer over U of S sweats. "But I still think you two are just no fun anymore."

The three of them were huddled in a phone booth on the edge of the parking lot beside President's Hall. Faith was crouched low, watching Christopher trot back and forth from the reception to the news van. KC stared, too, while Winnie examined the graffiti on the walls of the phone booth.

"I wonder why so many police are guarding the entrances," Faith observed.

"I don't know," KC snapped. She shuddered a little, then looked away. "The governor's supposed to be here."

"That's a lot of police just for a governor," said Winnie. "You'd think they were expecting Princess Diana." She squinted and put her face closer to the glass. "Hey, here's some guy's number. It says, call if you're looking for a good time. Maybe I should take him up on it. Anything would have to be better than Matthew the Dweeb."

"Winnie!"

"Just kidding, KC."

"I never know with you."

"KC, you know exactly what to expect from me. It's you two who are the mystery girls."

As KC and Winnie bantered, Faith wriggled past them and out of the booth. "I'll be right back, you guys. Don't leave without me."

"But I thought—"

"Faith!"

Faith was already jogging across the lot, barely listening to her friends. The police were watching her every move, but when they saw her head for the TV-news van rather than President's Hall itself, they relaxed and left her alone.

Faith stuck her head inside the van. "Christopher," she called.

Christopher was sorting through a mess of cables, cameras, and rolls of videotape. When he glanced up, he looked as if he expected to be yelled at. Faith had never seen such a cowed expression on his face.

When he recognized her, Christopher relaxed a little, then looked confused.

"Hi. It's me."

"What are you doing here?" He wiped his brow.

"I just wanted to see you, I guess."

Christopher huffed angrily. "I can't talk long, Faith. I'm working. Everybody's uptight because this reception is going to make such a boring piece. Plus every time we go in and out to get a microphone or a light, the cops want to check us out."

Faith wasn't sure what else to say. "I just thought we would get together today. And . . . I don't know, I wanted to find out what was going on—with us."

"You couldn't wait until tomorrow?"

"No. I don't even know if I'll see you tomorrow."

Christopher turned away and leaned into the van, while Faith put her hands to her face. What was she doing? She'd never been the demanding type with Brooks. One reason she'd broken up with Brooks was that he thought she needed to be taken care of. Had the insecurity of this relationship turned her into a needy, jealous wimp?

"Oh God, Christopher," she backtracked. "I'm sorry. I'm bugging you when you need to be concentrating on your work. I shouldn't have come here. I just . . ." She searched for words, trying to figure out what had made her come all the way across campus to spy on him. "I don't know. I'm sorry."

He kept sorting through the stuff in the van, avoiding her eyes. "Faith, I'm sorry about last night. But things like that are going to come up." He reached for a clipboard and started checking off a list of equipment. "You'll just have to trust me."

"You wouldn't lie to me, would you?"

It took a moment for him to answer. "Of course not. I would never lie to you."

"Okay. I do trust you," she said, trying to convince herself.

He gave her a quick kiss, then went back to his clipboard.

Faith backed away, glancing at KC and Winnie, who were still in the phone booth, waiting for her. She didn't feel any better.

* * *

Lauren had decided that no one could stop her from accomplishing her mission: Not Alison, not the police, not the regents, and certainly not her own fear.

But she hadn't thought about the two people who could make her heart seize up and her stomach lurch. She had never imagined that KC and Christopher Hammond would be there.

"Oh, God," she whispered.

KC was standing in the parking-lot phone booth with Winnie. And Christopher was beside the KRUS van, just having finished a conversation with Faith.

Hidden by a fir tree in the park across the street, Lauren reminded herself of what she needed to accomplish. Not only did she need to do it for Hilda Markman, she needed to do it for herself. Then she mulled over Alison's conclusion about an informer and her mind began to race.

Alison was probably right. Someone *had* ratted. Lauren was a little paranoid because she'd held onto her last message longer than she should have, even stowed it for a day in her writing journal. Still, she didn't think anyone else had seen it, unless Faith had read it in their mailbox or the privacy of their room. But even if Faith had accidentally seen it, she would never have told anyone. Faith wasn't a meddler.

Suddenly Lauren made the connection. KC! KC could have seen that message when she was delivering the dorm's mail. KC could have called the police out of deliberate malice and hatred for Lauren.

That thought made Lauren's pulse race and her heart throb. She was suddenly so angry that she wanted to run across the street and tackle KC to the ground. Whether KC was guilty or not, Lauren wanted to drag her back to the coalition members and make her tell them all the truth.

But the three friends were leaving, and Lauren couldn't get herself to budge. Rooted to the ground, she watched Faith, Winnie, and KC strolling in perfect step, heading away from the phone booth and President's Hall and back toward the dorms.

"What now?" Lauren asked herself.

She stared at Christopher and it came flooding back. Those few magical moments when she'd danced with him, actually believing that he was interested in her. And then the horrible, sickening fall when she'd found out it was a joke. It turned her stomach just to look at Christopher's tall, elegant frame, his auburn hair and handsome, preppy face. She had never, ever wanted to set eyes on Christopher Hammond again.

But just before Lauren turned her gaze away she saw the emblem on Christopher's nylon parka. She'd assumed it would say ODT, or U of S track, or the name of some play he'd directed for the drama department. But it said KRUS News. Lauren remembered Faith referring to Christopher's internship at the station.

The TV news! That was the answer. If Lauren could get KRUS to cover their demonstration, it wouldn't matter that the coalition couldn't get into the reception hall. If they got on the evening news, it wouldn't matter if they'd held their demonstration at the Springfield city dump.

Lauren looked at Christopher again and tried to pull together every ounce of courage from every secret place. Her legs felt as heavy as cast-iron posts, but she forced herself to cross the street. As she got closer and saw Christopher's graceful, lean profile, she almost turned back. Facing an entire police squad with pistols and nightsticks would have been easier than approaching Christopher Hammond again.

Nonetheless, she forced herself to step down off the curb, cross the parking lot, walk in front of all the campus cops, and tap Christopher on the shoulder.

Christopher spun around as if he didn't know whether he would get yelled at or blow his top himself. When he saw Lauren's face, he stared at her as if she were an alien.

"Do you remember me?" she managed.

"What?"

Lauren knew from his blank look that he had no idea who she was. It was ironic, since their "date" was something she would never, ever be able to forget.

"Your roommate set us up for the Trash your Roommate dance," she said bluntly.

He finally nodded, then rubbed his eyes, as if it were an evening he didn't want to remember, either.

"That doesn't matter, though." She took a deep breath. Surprisingly, she had no desire to turn back now. "What matters is that the Progressive Students' Coalition wanted to stage a peaceful demonstration tonight, protesting the destruction of Bickford Lane." Lauren was amazed to hear her voice come out so clear and strong. "But the police won't let us into the hall. Can you give us any time on the newscast, anyway? A mention, a single shot, anything that would help get our message out?"

Christopher's face lit up. "How many people are there?" he said, pulling away from the van and looking around.

"Over twenty. Everyone else is waiting back in the park. We have a whole event planned, with posters and dramatic scenes."

Christopher's eyes got even bigger. He took her wrist and kissed her hand. "You're wonderful," he gushed. "Wait right here."

Christopher raced across the parking lot and disappeared into President's Hall. A moment later he came back with two older men and a woman, all of whom wore KRUS identification badges. They descended on Lauren with great interest while the cops looked on.

"Some students want to do a demonstration?" asked the older man.

"That's right. A dramatic demonstration against the destruction of Bickford Lane," Lauren said quickly. "But the police won't let us into the building because it's a private party."

"So why don't you do it out here?" The older man winked, then gave Christopher a pat. "Good thinking, young man." He smiled at his co-workers. "Let's bring all our equipment outside," he instantly ordered. "I think we finally have something for the eleven o'clock news!" He looked back at Lauren. "Can you get your friends to demonstrate just across the street, on the edge of the park?"

Lauren was already running back across the street. "We'll all be here in five minutes!"

She flew back to the tennis courts, praying that Dash and the others were still there. When she found them it looked like Alison and Richard were about to leave, while Dash was trying to convince everyone else to stick around.

"I told you she'd come back," Dash cried.

"Well?"

"Could you do anything?"

"What happened?"

Lauren grabbed Dash's hand and pulled him back across the park. "Follow me," she called joyfully. "Bring all the stuff and hurry to the other side of the park!"

The coalition members slowly followed. They didn't pick up speed until they reached the edge of the park and saw the TV crew waiting for them.

"You did this?" Dash asked, looking at Lauren with astonishment and awe.

Before Lauren could answer, there were shouts in the night.

"Let's do it!"

"Lights!"
"Camera!"
The tape of Hilda Markman's voice blared as the lights flashed and the cameras began to roll.

Thirteen

hey drove in silence, past dew-covered lawns and over downtown streets that were coming to life with Monday-morning traffic. The farther they got from the university, the grittier and grimier the buildings became. At last Steven pulled up in front of Bernhard's Wholesale Athletic Supply, a low brick warehouse on a gray, dead-end street. He parked his Corvette and for a moment he and KC sat, listening to the rumble of talk radio and staring straight ahead.

"Do we have everything we need?"

KC became even more contained and cool. These were the first words they'd spoken to each other since Steven had picked her up at the dining commons.

"I have a copy of the contract and a list of all our soccer-shirt orders." She took a fat envelope out of her briefcase and slapped it on the dash. It was the money she'd withdrawn from the soccer account the previous Thursday. "Here's all the cash from our account. It's almost three hundred dollars short."

Steven reached for his wallet. "I'll cover that."

"I'll pay you back," KC responded icily.

"You don't have to, partner. I can spare it."

"I don't need charity."

"I didn't say you did."

"I'll pay you back."

"Fine. Pay me back."

"Thank you."

Steven extracted the extra money from his wallet and slipped it in the envelope. Then he turned off the radio. Neither of them moved.

"Is Helen meeting us?" KC asked in the most businesslike manner she could manage. Helen was an older woman who had returned to finish her degree and was one of their partners from class. She was helping to deliver the shirts to the dorms. "All those shirts will never fit in this car."

"I know." Steven looked around his Corvette, at the elaborate radio, the custom leather seats.

"I talked to Helen last night. She'll be here at seven-thirty with her station wagon."

"Good," KC said, holding back everything she was thinking and feeling. "Let's get this over with." She climbed out in her blazer and skirt, swinging her briefcase, and walked up Bernhard's front steps. A moment later she heard Steven's car door slam and the *clap clap* of his loafers as he followed her inside.

When they were at the reception desk, KC really looked at Steven for the first time that morning. She felt a ping of shock. There were circles under his eyes. Even though his shirt and khaki slacks had been ironed, he looked frazzled. His face had a distracted look, and he stood with his shoulders slumped.

"We're here to pick up the U of S shirt order," KC said to the receptionist. "The name of our company is Soccer, Inc."

The woman smiled and pointed to marked boxes stacked near the front door. She plucked an invoice off the top of her desk while Steven pulled out the envelope and counted the cash. KC looked away.

And then it was over. The money had been paid and the shirts were theirs to deliver to the players on the intramural dorm teams. The transaction that KC had been dreading for weeks had been completed as effortlessly as if they'd just gone to the Seven-Eleven and picked up a quart of milk. But KC felt no relief. She felt nothing, except a fleeting hope that maybe she'd finally be able to sleep, to study, to concentrate without numbers flipping through her head.

When KC and Steven got back outside, Helen was waiting in her big, clunky station wagon with Edward, the international student who was their fourth business-class partner. Edward helped load the boxes into Helen's car and soon he and Helen took off, heading back to the university while KC and Steven climbed back into the Corvette.

Steven started the car while KC reached for the radio, unable to face the silence again. But then Steven turned the engine off. He slumped forward with his arms across the steering wheel and stared out across the busy street.

"We're supposed to meet Helen and Edward back at the dorms," KC stated. "We really should get going. The rush-hour traffic is going to start getting bad."

"You blow me away, partner," Steven exhaled. "When I first met you I knew you were something. But I didn't know you were this tough. You just blow me away."

KC sat as still and rigid as a slab of steel.

"Look, Steven, we went out a few times, we worked on a project together, and it didn't work out. Let's just go back to the dorms and not make a big deal out of it. Okay?"

"Yeah, right," he came back. "It's no big deal. It's nothing at all, what happened between us. It doesn't mean anything that you cried in my arms. Knowing you, you probably cry on the shoulder of every guy you go out with, right?"

KC tried not to fall apart. Maybe she'd cried for Steven once, but she wasn't about to do it again.

"It doesn't mean anything that I made you laugh, Little Angel. Or that we kissed."

KC stared straight ahead.

Steven pounded the steering wheel. "Okay. It doesn't even mean anything that you stole from our soccer account and didn't tell me about it."

KC could no longer stay cool. She faced him furiously. "I knew you'd use that against me and that's why I didn't want to tell you. All right, I made a mistake. I admit it. I wanted to impress you with great clothes and this great image, so I charged too much on my credit card and then I couldn't pay it off. But at least I didn't use you, Steven. I knew you could have paid off that debt for me, that all I had to do was ask you for the money. But I didn't want to use you the way you decided to use me."

"I used you? How did I use you?"

"You were the one who had to show your important father what a pathetic, lowlife girl you were dating. You were the one who had to parade me in front of your dad so that he could know you didn't care at all what he thinks or says."

"Is that what you think?"

"I'm not stupid, Steven. That's what I *know.*"

"I've never thought you were anything but very, very smart, partner—until now." Steven wiped a hand across his tired face. "You thought I was using you to bug my father? Are you kidding? My father thought you were the greatest thing since the invention of the automobile. He's never been so impressed. I had breakfast with him yesterday and he wouldn't shut up about you, about how you were a go-getter, how you were just like him. He's sure that you're going to be an incredible success."

"Me?"

"Sure. I'm the one he's worried about. I'm the one he thinks is pathetic. I wasn't using you, KC. I admit I acted like a jerk at dinner, but it's not because I think you're some kind of lowlife. It's because I was jealous of you! My father was treating you the way I want him to treat me."

KC finally looked into Steven's eyes and saw that deep hurt she'd seen after the dinner with Steven's father. She wanted to start over, to take it all back—the business project, the insults, the teasing, the feud with Lauren, the dinner with his dad. But she knew that wasn't possible. To really start over, she'd have to go a lot further back than the day she'd first met Steven Garth. "Maybe we're just not good for each other."

He moved closer and touched her cheek. "Why do you say that, partner?"

KC was suddenly overwhelmed by his closeness, his sadness, and the realization that she still cared for him. In spite of herself, she put her hand on top of his. Tears came to her eyes. "What happened between us won't go away. I think we're just too different to stay together. Steven, I just don't think you bring out the best in me. Our business project is almost over, and pretty soon we won't even be partners anymore."

He pulled back to look at her face again, then kissed her. One short, sweet, goodbye kiss. Everything inside KC melted for that brief, close moment.

"This is sad, Little Angel." Steven caught a single tear as it ran down KC's cheek. "Because the problem isn't that we're too different. The problem is that we're too much alike."

* * *

When Winnie got to film class later that morning, there were a few surprises waiting on her chair: a bouquet of daisies, some caramels in a little heart-shaped box, and a copy of *E.T.* rented from the local video store.

"How can this guy still like me?" she muttered to herself as she looked around for Matthew. But before she could make a good survey of the hall, the lights went down and their professor started showing a film he referred to as a grand disaster. It was called *Acting From the Heart.*

As the screen came to life and she stretched out in her seat, Winnie thought about all the grand disasters that had happened to her and her friends since they'd arrived at U of S. Had they been acting from their hearts? Maybe Faith was acting from her heart, but Winnie still had a feeling that something was very wrong. She would never say anything about it to Faith, but she suspected that something about fabulous Christopher wasn't quite on the up-and-up.

And KC. Winnie knew that part of KC was crazy about Steven, but that she was about to end things with him anyway. Only Lauren seemed to be acting from the heart lately. Only shy, sheltered Lauren seemed to be doing what she really wanted to do.

As Winnie watched the movie, which was full of music and surreal effects, she had to wonder about herself as well. Since running into Josh during homecoming weekend, she'd only seen him once, in the dining commons, where he'd been eating breakfast alone. She'd wanted to sit with him so badly she almost tripped over her duck shoes. She'd sensed that he'd wanted to talk to her, too. He'd smiled and waved her over, but she'd deliberately ignored him. It was as if Winnie had wanted to prove to Josh that she didn't care; that even though she was a flake, she expected him to be Mr. Normal; that making plans and formal dates were more important than how she felt deep in her heart.

"Speaking of Mr. Normal . . . or rather, Mr. Classically Weird," Winnie muttered as the film came to an end and she saw Matthew was waiting for her after all. He had scooted out into the aisle, and was standing right at the end of her row.

Winnie had had such a lousy time with him the day before that she hadn't expected ever to speak to him again. She couldn't believe he hadn't gotten the message from her deader-than-dead kiss. Getting up from her seat, she held up the flowers, the candy, and the video. "Is this all from you?"

Matthew walked beside her in Chinese canvas shoes and karate pants. "Who else?"

"You didn't need to do this."

"I had such a good time yesterday that I wanted to do something." He grinned and tossed back his rattail. "The video's due back tomorrow by exactly five."

"Okay."

He followed her out into the foyer and down the hall, where he stopped and took out his appointment book. "I planned what we're going to do next Saturday. There's a taffy tasting at this candy store downtown, and then they're showing a whole day of old horror films at the Dogwood Cinema. In between I thought you could go with me to drop in on the film critic for the *Springfield Bee.* I've been calling her every day for an appointment."

"This coming Saturday?" This was a new one for Winnie. She'd always been the one who didn't get the message, who stayed in there long after the other person lost interest. She'd been the dumpee so many times that she assumed being the dumper was easy. She was surprised to find her tongue tied and her voice sticking in her throat. "Actually, Matthew, um, I can't. I'm sorry."

"You can't on Saturday? How about Sunday?"

"Sorry. I need to study. Midterms are coming up."

"Friday night?"

Winnie moved aside to let some grad students pass. "Friday night is out, too."

He looked confused. Finally a flicker of realization passed over his face. "Oh. Did I do something wrong?"

Winnie thought of all the things she could say. *I don't like you, Matthew. You're a bore. You don't listen. I can't handle having every second of my life planned out.* But she didn't want to hurt him. And yet she didn't want to lie. "The truth is, Matthew," she heard herself say. "I'm interested in someone else."

Matthew's face went blank, and then he plastered on a fake smile. "Oh, I see. Okay. I understand."

"You do?"

"Of course. It's classic." He pointed to the candy and flowers. "You can keep that stuff, though, if you want."

"Thank you."

"Just remember to take the video back."

"I will."

"By five o'clock."

"I won't forget."

He backed away. "Okay. Uh, see you around."

Winnie stood in the hall and smiled. Maybe things with Josh would never work out. Maybe she was a fool to stay interested in him. But no matter what, she realized, she had to follow her heart.

Fourteen

"**I** can't believe we didn't see this on the news last night," said Faith, crowding around Lauren's TV in their dorm room with Winnie, KC, and most of the Coleridge Hall freshmen. "How did we miss it?"

"We didn't watch the news last night," Winnie reminded her. She turned around and grinned at Lauren. "I'm so glad you taped it for us, Lauren. It would have been a total drag not to have seen it. Don't you think so, KC?"

KC didn't answer. She was standing in the corner of the room, surrounded by other freshmen who all seemed to be wearing leotards or painter's smocks. KC seemed to be the only one not thrilled with the picture on the TV screen.

Lauren waited until the clip was over. No matter how many times she'd seen it, she was astounded at the sight of herself, Dash, and the other coalition members on TV. Their demonstration had been featured on the previous night's eleven o'clock news. The anchors had made it their big story of the newscast, with almost four minutes of coverage.

When the videotape was finished, Lauren looked over at KC and repeated, "KC is definitely glad she didn't miss seeing our demonstration. Aren't you, KC?"

"I have to go," KC snapped, pushing her way through the artsy crowd.

"Don't leave, KC," Winnie cried out. "We have to go over the next chapter for Western Civ."

"Stay here," Faith agreed. "As soon as this is rewound we can study and then go to dinner together." Faith reached to punch the button on the VCR.

There was a wail of objection from the Coleridge group.

"Let's watch it one more time."

"This is better than my drama class."

"I love the stage blood."

"Lauren, I can't believe you all had the guts to do this."

"I'm so glad you did do it. It's horrible that the regents want to tear those houses down."

"Play it once more!"

KC pushed her way toward the door. She called back to Faith and Winnie, "I still have a few more soccer shirts to deliver. I'll find you at dinner."

Lauren tore herself away from the repeat showing and ran after KC. She didn't catch up to her until they were both in the Coleridge lobby. A girl was practicing on the lobby piano, but Lauren didn't concern herself with her. She rushed in front of KC, fiercely blocking her exit.

Lauren grabbed KC's arm. "Surprised to see what an effect our demonstration had?" she asked.

"What do you mean by that?" KC pulled away from her and tried to get out the door.

Lauren had a brief flash of doubt. What if it hadn't been KC? "Don't act so innocent," she bluffed.

"Lauren, I don't know what you're talking about."

"Oh, come on. Your mail job made it easy for you to open people's mail."

"I never opened anyone's mail," KC shot back.

"But I can't help it if not every note and letter is sealed in an envelope."

Lauren smiled. "So you did see my message, didn't you? And then you told the police about our plans."

KC's face turned pale. "You're crazy."

"It had to be you!" Lauren went on. "Is it easier to lie or just to keep your mouth shut?"

KC winced. She knew Lauren was referring to the fact that although KC had known Lauren was being set up for the fraternity prank, she had done nothing to warn her. KC tried to get out the door one more time. But when Lauren stopped her again, she gasped and put a hand over her mouth. "All right," she muttered.

"It was you," Lauren said sadly.

"How did you find out?"

"I guessed."

KC slammed her fist against the door. "What are you going to do about it? Put me before your fellow demonstrators and let them shoot me?"

Lauren had always been so impressed with KC's beauty and smarts. She'd wanted her friendship so badly and had been so devastated when it hadn't worked out. But as she stared at KC in the harsh lobby light, she saw someone who was just as scared as she used to be.

"Why, KC? Why did you do it?"

"I don't know!" KC shouted, finally getting past Lauren and hurrying out into the night. "I don't know why I do a lot of things."

And then she was gone. Lauren leaned against the big window and stared out at the dark green while the pianist finished her practice session. When at last the musician packed up her music and closed the piano, Lauren left, too.

Lauren went right to the dorm parking lot and unlocked her BMW, which was still full of placards left over from the protest. She drove off campus. Within minutes she was out of her car again, and standing in front of the Tri Beta house on Sorority Row.

The regular Monday night dinner was going on, a required event for all active and pledging members. Lauren was late. She'd decided to show up only because she'd gotten a phone message that afternoon from Courtney Conner, personally requesting Lauren's presence at the sorority house that night.

As Lauren walked over the pristine front lawn and saw the soft light filtering through the lacy curtains, she knew that something was up. Monday dinners were the most routine of Greek events. Pledges didn't get reminder calls, especially from their house president. Lauren had forced the Tri Betas to the breaking point. All

her sins had added up: she'd missed the first decorating session, dressed like a bohemian, shown
up with Dash at the homecoming open house,
skipped the secret-sister session, and, finally, appeared on the evening news as part of a radical
protest. Short of bombing the sorority house,
she didn't know what else she could do to get
herself kicked out.

Excited and terrified, Lauren opened the front
door and walked into the house.

The sisters and pledges were already eating dinner on tables decorated with fall leaves and rust-
colored ribbons. As soon as Lauren walked into
the dining room, every pretty head turned in her
direction.

"Please sit down, Lauren," Courtney announced, standing up and tapping a spoon
against a crystal goblet. "We saved you some dinner." She patted the empty chair right next to
hers.

Lauren slowly walked up to the place next to
Courtney as if she were approaching the gallows.
It was so quiet that she could hear the squeak of
the sandals she'd borrowed from Winnie as she
crossed the well-finished wooden floor.

"Sorry I'm late," she whispered, obeying some
old reflex.

"That's all right," Courtney said in her

smooth, commanding voice. "We all know what a busy weekend you had."

Lauren sat down and checked out the sisters' faces again. Most of them stared at her as if she were some bizarre curiosity. They were probably all thinking how relieved they were not to be in her shoes. Marielle's face was pinched with disgust.

Food was passed to her. Lauren dumped a few spoonfuls on her plate but was unable to touch a single bite. She waited for the next announcement—the eviction proceeding, the boot.

Courtney remained standing. She tapped her goblet one more time, requesting attention. When every pair of eyes was gazing up at her, she began her speech.

Lauren stared down at her plate.

"As a sisterhood," Courtney lectured, "we need to recognize a girl who stands out, who does something different."

Lauren steeled herself.

"We sometimes forget that service to our community is one of our sorority's goals," Courtney went on. "It's easy for us to get so caught up in our social events that we forget that one of our reasons for existing is to improve the community in which we live. That's why I wanted to present

Lauren as an example of someone we should admire."

Lauren lifted her head. She wasn't sure she had heard correctly.

Courtney smiled down at her. "Lauren stood up for something she believes in and committed herself to helping others. That's what being a Tri Beta is all about. Lauren, do you have anything to add?"

Lauren was so shocked that she could have fallen in her mashed potatoes. Blankly, she shook her head and then looked from face to tastefully made-up face, realizing that what she'd taken for scorn was actually admiration and respect.

"I don't have anything to add," Lauren managed. "Thank you."

"Thank *you.*" Courtney sat down. "That's all, everyone. Enjoy dessert."

There was a smattering of applause and, one by one, girls began leaning across the table to address Lauren.

"We saw you on the news."

"I never realized that the regents did terrible things like that. You are so brave."

"We saw your friend Dash on the news, too."

"Lauren, he is really sexy."

"I thought he was great when I met him at the

open house, but then when I saw him on TV, I couldn't believe it."

Two pledges pretended to faint, and fell, giggling, into each other's arms.

Lauren couldn't believe it either. Only when she met Marielle's eyes and recognized that old contempt was she reminded of what had gone on in the house and how much she still wanted to get kicked out.

But for that night, she wasn't making any progress. If anything, her mother would only have more support for her opinion that the Tri Beta sorority was the ideal place for Lauren to be.

Still hoping to offend someone besides Marielle, Lauren excused herself early. But once again, Courtney was all too understanding.

"Of course," Courtney cooed, walking Lauren to the door. "You must be tired after a weekend like that." They stopped in the doorway. "By the way," Courtney added, "thank you for putting those croissants in my room as my secret homecoming sister. My roommate saw you sneaking out one morning, so I found out that it was you. With everything else you've been doing lately, I appreciate you taking the time to stay so committed to our house."

Feeling as if she were in the middle of some

absurdist play, Lauren said goodnight and walked back toward her car.

She might have felt as if her whole life were unreal, as if even the protest had been some silly sham, had she not seen a rugged figure leaning against her BMW. He was smoking a cigarette and scratching a day's growth of beard in a puddle of light under the street lamp.

Slowly, Lauren walked up to Dash. "Hi."

He nodded. "I wanted to tell you something," he said. "I stopped by your dorm and your roommate said you were usually here on Monday nights." He gestured toward the Tri Beta house. "I didn't want to go in that place again. I saw your car and decided to wait. Nice night."

"Yes." Lauren looked up at the starry sky and laughed.

"What's funny?"

"Nothing. Just my split personality again. What did you want to tell me?"

Dash smiled. "That the regents backed down."

"What?"

"Yeah. They got so many phone calls today that they changed their minds about tearing down Bickford Lane. Alison just found out. There'll be a press release tomorrow."

"No parking lot?"

"Nope."

"Hilda Markman can stay in her house?"

"That's right. We won, Lauren. We won!"

"We won!" Without thinking, Lauren threw her arms around Dash's neck. The next thing she knew, he was hugging her and they were both half jumping, half dancing in the street. And then they were very still, just holding each other, breathing at the same time and feeling the contour of each other's body, the texture of each other's skin.

When they separated, they both laughed a little and didn't know what to say.

"We did it," Dash finally whispered.

"We did."

Neither of them moved, but Dash's eyes took in every inch of her face. His mouth lifted in the sweetest smile, and his dark eyes looked happy.

Lauren wanted to leap for joy. No one had ever looked at her like that before.

But how could they have? Lauren had just become an entirely new person.

Here's a sneak preview of
Freshman Nights, *the fourth*
book in the compelling story
of FRESHMAN DORM.

As soon as Faith looked outside, her heart sped up and her breath momentarily stopped.

"Christopher!" Faith cried.

There he was, leaning against the drinking fountain as if he were part of the landscape. Lean and auburn haired, he was wearing a crisp blue shirt with the sleeves rolled up, dark slacks, and a striped tie. He looked like a handsome TV news anchor, and he had probably just come from his intern job at the TV station. Seeing him, Faith was relieved and incredibly happy at the same time. Every time she saw him lately, she wondered if she would ever lay eyes on him again.

"Faith!"

At once they were laughing and kissing and wrapping themselves in each others' arms. They flowed from strong hugs to light kisses, then into a slow, wonderful moment where they just looked into one anothers' eyes.

"What are you doing here?" Faith asked.

"Waiting for you." He grinned. "I haven't seen you for so long."

"Four days. Where have you been?"

He kissed her again. "You know how busy I get."

She looked away, trying not to think about Suzanna Pennerman. "I know."

"I just wanted to see you. I *had* to see you. I had to tell you something."

Faith reached for him again, and then all thought went out of her head. It all came down to touch—soft hands, warm skin, and silky hair. His arms slipped around her waist, hers around his neck, and they were kissing, right there in the middle of MacLaughlin Park.

They might not have stopped, except that Faith finally remembered her job at the day-care center. "I've got to go," she whispered.

Christopher nodded.

Still, neither of them took a step away. Lately, Faith wanted to be so close to Christopher that it scared her. Every sober thought in her sensible head said that he was not the kind of guy for her. Sure, he was charming, successful, and smart, but Faith couldn't forget that Christopher was also cheating on his fiancée. Worse, Christopher was never around when Faith really needed him.

"It's crazy always having to worry about who might see us," Faith admitted.

"I know." Christopher brushed back a wisp of her hair. "But maybe it won't be like this all the time."

"Really?"

He smiled and looked off at the line of birch trees that rimmed the park.

Faith rested her cheek against his shoulder. As exciting as all the secrecy was, it also hurt to be the girl on the side. Christopher showed up as if by magic whenever he felt like seeing her, but Faith never surprised him. Their relationship had unwritten rules, and one was that she should never pop up at his track workout or his TV apprentice job. She'd never even been to ODT, his fraternity house, and other than their drama crowd, she'd never met any of his friends.

Christopher glanced around to make sure they were still alone and spoke more softly. "Faith, I talked to my friend Jamie, the guy I told you about."

"You did?" Faith's heart began to pump so fast that she felt unsteady.

"That's what I wanted to tell you." Christopher smiled. "Jamie's going away to an athletic conference. If we really want to be together and not have to worry about other people, we could go up to his cabin next Wednesday night."

Jamie was a track buddy of Christopher's who lived in an isolated mountain cabin about ten miles out of town. Christopher had mentioned going up to the cabin before. Nothing had been spelled out, but Faith knew what going would mean. What she didn't know was how that would change their relationship. Their relationship certainly needed to change. She wanted to know that Christopher would be close and safe and there when she needed him.

"What do you think?" Christopher whispered, pulling her close again.

Faith was unable to think.

"I think it would be great not to worry about being found out every two seconds," Christopher added. "We could really be alone."

The idea of being alone with Christopher made Faith feel dizzy. But a moment later, the painful tightness came back. She imagined not seeing Christopher at all until Sunday, not exchanging a hello, and then going to the cabin.

"Faith," Christopher persisted, "what do you think?"

Christopher touched Faith's chin, making her tip her face up to look at him. "What's the matter?"

Faith wanted to tell him a hundred different things. *I don't trust you. I may be in love with you, but I'm scared. If I take such a big step, and go to the cabin with you, what kind of commitment will I get from you in return?*

"What about Suzanna?" she finally mumbled.

"Faith, forget about Suzanna," Christopher urged. "Suzanna and I will be over soon. It's just you and me. You're the one that matters. We should go to Jamie's cabin and be together."

"You're right," Faith finally whispered, and then she was in his arms again.